THE LITTLE KAROO

Reproduced from a conté crayon drawing by Peter Lamb, inscribed "For Ethel Campbell from Pauline Smith, August 12th 1935", owned by the "Campbell Collections" of the University of Natal.

THE LITTLE KAROO

BY

PAULINE SMITH

With a Foreword by
GUY BUTLER

an Introduction by
ARNOLD BENNETT

and a Preface by
WILLIAM PLOMER

A.A.BALKEMA/CAPE TOWN

1981

FIRST PUBLISHED IN 1925

THIS NEW EDITION PUBLISHED IN 1981

BY ARRANGEMENT WITH JONATHAN CAPE LIMITED

By the same author

Platkops Children
The Beadle

ISBN 0 86961 1305

CONTENTS

CONTENTS

FOREWORD

The title invites us to see the work as regional: and regional it is in evocation of heat and space, of niggardly grey plains alternating with valleys in whose groins shine small homesteads, green fields and orchards, with an occasional water mill, or a focal white-washed church.

But since the mid-twenties that space has been defeated by the railway bus and the motor car, and the inner *lebensraum* of its people invaded by the vulgarities of chain stores, consumerism, Springbok Radio and S.A.T.V. By 1940 the class from which most of her characters are drawn—the Poor Whites—had all but ceased to exist in the countryside. A book such as Yvonne Burgess's *A Life to Live* (Johannesburg 1971) gives some idea of what their migration into the cities could entail, and makes the important observation that rural poverty is seldom as squalid as urban.

But it would be a mistake, having discovered an arcadian archetype behind these stories, to rest in it. Nowhere does our author invite us to think in idyllic terms. On the contrary, she creates with a striking insistence, beneath the lucidly sketched landscape of every story, the shimmer of a biblical desert that can blossom as the rose. How could it be otherwise? That is what her characters saw.

It was not any obsession with the Karoo landscape that impelled her to write: it was devotion to the people who inhabited it:
"I always felt that what had been written about them did not do them full justice, and I made up my mind to write about them as I had known them".
Again, after writing her masterpiece, *The Pain*,
". . . A sense of failure oppressed me. Again it seemed to me that I failed to do justice to these people as I saw them —so fine in their simplicity, so courageous in their poverty."
"to do justice to these people." Who were they?

vii

She tells us that "The Dutch farmers among whom my father's work as a doctor lay, still lived in primitive simplicity close to God. Among these people we had many friends, and all their way of life, and their slow and brooding talk which fell so naturally into the English of the Old Testament, was full of interest to us".

It is true that there is a greater similarity between the English of the King James Version of the Old Testament and Afrikaans than there is between the English of the 19th century novel and Afrikaans; and there are indeed phrases and idioms in the sometimes quaint English of these stories which are self-conscious Afrikanerisms. To stop here, however, is to be satisfied with an explanation of certain incidentals of her style, not its essentials.

There is far more to the English of the Old Testament, or indeed any translation of the Old Testament, than this; and more attention should be given to the narrative style of that great book, which exerts such a formative force on the lives and speech of her characters, and on the entire style of *The Little Karoo*. What, for instance, distinguishes it from much of the meticulously accurate description in some South African writing of the social realist school?

I suspect it is her subtle integration of the temporal circumstances of her characters with their ultimate destiny. Whatever we may think, they think their souls are immortal; and their belief in an eternal background suffuses the foreground with a significance not found in merely graphic description. Her method of characterisation is by ontological predicament, rather than by class dynamics or psychological determinism.

Her stories have closer affinities with compact forms like the old ballad and drama than with the discursive novel. Her imagination seizes upon extreme situations in the approaches to death. Indeed, a bare outline of these stories might suggest that she had a morbid addiction to the more lurid and melodramatic happenings of the community. But, as in good tragedies and ballads, the violent incident is merely the generator of the agonies and triumphs of souls put to the final test by some terrible crisis.

Her preoccupation with the tragic had to be endured, no matter what the short term consequences for her writing. "I wrote with little hope of publication for we (Arnold Bennett & herself) both believed that no editor . . . would accept stories so uniformly tragic as those of *The Little Karoo* —and I knew I could write no others until my mind was relieved of the burden of these."

She wrote them slowly, painfully, and, above all, with truth to a vision which was compassionate without being sentimental. The patience which her long illnesses had taught her entered into her art. She would refuse to force a story because her understanding of human experience forbade its reduction to sequences of interesting incidents fabricated to make moral or social points.

"I could not *make* situations to suit the needs of a story as a story—all I could do was to describe, often after long waiting, the slow development in the lives of my characters which lay outside my will."

Her prime consideration, then, was to do justice to her characters' experience; and those characters saw themselves as fallen creatures living under a God whose justice was harsh and whose mercy was mysterious. Her own determination to do justice to them is bound up with their own concern with justice; and her compassionate stance is related to the mercy which demands that we should forgive as we need be forgiven:

" 'God forgive me, Niklaas, if I should judge you, for there is not one of us who has not sinned.' . . . and then it was as if in pity and forgiveness God Himself had spoken." *The Sinner.*

Character after character grows, and is pruned, or hacked, into that unique shape which bears the tragic fruit: ripeness is all.

Some do not, of course, bear such fruit—like Alie's son in *Desolation*—"a weak and obstinate man who saw in his God a power actively engaged in direct opposition to himself, and at each blow dealt to him by his God, he lifted up his voice and cried aloud in his injury." Or the tuberculotic Miller, who refuses the ancient benisons of contrition and humility offered by the Pastor:

"Is it by gifts alone that a man shall be judged? Surely not, my children . . . The sacrifices to God are a broken spirit: a broken and contrite heart He will not despise."

He dies dumbly fumbling a belated gesture of love towards his wife, in whose arms he is allowed to die. Similarly, the most sadistic and insane of these sufferers, whose obsession with God's injustice drives him to attempt the murder of his own son, dies in the arms of the young woman who has stopped him.

"The stricken man looked up at the son . . . who had thus, to the last, eluded him—but speech was beyond him. So, too, perhaps, was hatred. So too, perhaps, were bitterness and unjust suspicion . . . All that was known and could afterwards be told was that, with his last conscious movement, it was towards Dientje and away from his son that he turned —and under her compassionate gaze that he closed his eyes upon the world." *The Father.*

It is no accident that Pauline Smith chose to end the volume with this cautious yet unequivocal suggestion of the redeeming power of compassion.

We return, then, to what many critics regard as the great achievement of this book: the creation of the landscape of an entire region. No one will question Pauline Smith's powers of description. It is the weight given to this aspect of her work which needs adjustment. As Ridley Beeton has observed, the book received its regional character almost by accident.

"Bennett realised, quite suddenly, that one of the defects of her work was that it had, in the assumption of its truthfulness, concerned itself too little with conveying a sense of locality to those who did not know the Karoo. He advised her to try to produce not a greater authenticity (for this was always there), but the better communication of a setting. Her short story, *The Pain*, one of her undoubted masterpieces, was the result." *Unisa English Studies*, Vol. XI, No. 1, March 1973 p. 42.

It would be interesting to know what, if any, additions of detail she made to the settings of the already written stories once *The Adelphi's* acceptance of *The Pain* had broken the publisher's ice.

On one thing one may be sure: no addition would have been made which falsified that "landscape of the mind" which her characters inhabited: Karoo in the foreground, biblical in its symbolical depths; a landscape so simplified and intensified that the profound moral mathematics of their beings, and of ours, becomes ruthlessly, mercifully, clearer.

GUY BUTLER
GRAHAMSTOWN
1981

PREFACE

A QUARTER of a century has passed since Arnold
Bennett wrote the introduction to this book, which
I read when it first appeared. As a writer of a later
generation, I count it a privilege to try and supple-
ment after so many years the remarks of a critic
so lively, sensible, independent, and outspoken. He
had at times the power to encourage young writers
when their own diffidence or the apathy or hostility
of others was against them; and anything he may have
done for this book of Pauline Smith's is the more to
be honoured, since it contains the best collection of
short stories yet written in English on South African
themes. In the appreciation of them I have one or
two advantages over Bennett: for instance, that when
young I lived for a time in that Cape Province which
includes the Little Karoo, and that to me the concept
of a South African literature is not so far-fetched as
it might have been to him.

Pauline Smith's stories are about people belonging
to the ethnic group variously known as the South
African Dutch (or just 'the Dutch'), the Boers, or
the Afrikaners. Her characters may be presumed to be
living in the first decade or two of the present century.
They live on the land without such mechanical aids
as motor-cars, radios, or telephones. They do not
travel far from home, and they do not seem to read
newspapers, talk politics, or bother at all about
the rest of the world: this story-teller's concern, it is
true, is chiefly with what goes on in their hearts.
Alone with their thoughts, they feel that 'Man is

distant, but God is near'—a phrase from Thomas Pringle, the first poet of South Africa. The God that presides over them is a stern Protestant god, a Dutch reformed god made in the image of men living a patriarchal pastoral life in many ways coloured by the Old Testament, and suggestive of it, a life in which the family and the land, and the work of the family upon the land, are the main concerns.

In the Stormberg in the early nineteen-twenties I knew people who lived the lives of Pauline Smith's characters, but I do not know how commonly it is still possible in South Africa to maintain such isolation. I do not know whether it is still possible in those sunburnt solitudes to descry, miles and miles away, the spiral pillar of dust that accompanies the white-hooded, jogging Cape-cart on its unhurried journey from a drowsy dorp to an almost secret farm, or the still more slowly moving pillar rising like gold dust in the golden air from some ponderous wagon drawn by sixteen oxen yoked in pairs. I imagine that there are still families of farmers and *bijwoners* with elbow-room and wonderfully restricted interests, still 'poor whites' as remote from flashy Johannesburg in their poverty and simple-mindedness as the veld-flower is from the stock-jobber: but the way of the world is against them because it is against isolation. Even if the life reflected in these stories is far more typical of forty years ago than of today, this does not mean that they are, in any unfavourable sense, 'dated'. It is indeed a great advantage to a fictionist to be able to write about an isolated community with, as Bennett put it, 'the most rigid standards of conduct—from which standards the human nature in them is continually falling away'.

The homogeneity of such a group of people at once imposed one kind of unity on any writing about them; every falling away from those rigid standards is of itself dramatic; and the concentration of family life leads to strains and crises which are the more significant and the more deeply felt since there is so little to distract attention from them. Relationships that go wrong are haunted by the ghost of the purpose—deflected, maimed, perverted, or extinguished—that they were to go right; life, though it may be lived at a slow pace, is lived with the whole being; nothing is cheapened; and under that huge clean sky it is, or was, easier to be wicked than vulgar. These stories are a reminder that a life 'narrow in its setting, harsh in its poverty' may allow, as it did to Dientje Mostert, dignity and grace: 'narrow' is the important word—one would not over-hopefully look for those qualities nowadays in an overcrowded urban proletariat.

The intelligent reader can dismiss any suspicion that the somewhat biblical simplicity of these stories suggests them to be the work of a writer who sees life in terms too plain and elemental. There is no lack of subtlety in Pauline Smith's understanding of human nature. She shows us 'The Pastor's Daughter' conscious that love can be 'beautiful and cruel and selfish and bitter, and who can tell where the one begins and the other ends?' She does not, like some facile idealists, dodge the fact that pugnacity is an attribute of the human male—of Piet Pienaar, for example, for whom 'battle was the natural means of intercourse with his fellow-men'. She can face the truth, even when it takes the form of a paranoiac miser; and she can thrust deeply into the truth, as

in that appalling glimpse of the father who 'sought
fiercely to wound, and so to reach and possess, the
mind of his son'. Or she can show how much, in
these narrow settings in the wide veld, small, choice
possessions may mean to their owners: Deltje's shell-
covered box goes with her like a talisman, and upon
Koba Nooi's shell-framed looking-glass has come to
depend her very technique of seduction.

The nearer Pauline Smith comes to the themes of
death or disaster—as in 'The Pain' or 'Desolation'
—the nearer to poetry is her presentation of human
nature in the face of these things. When Anna
Coetzee is discovered feverishly turning the handle
of that broken musical box, the symbolism of this
situation may be a trifle emphatic, but it is none the
less poetically true and whatever we are meant, in
'Ludovitje', to read into the revelation that only
Maqwasi the Kaffir can dig the graves of white Piet
and his wife, it has great force, like something in an
epic legend. It is to be noted that when, in this same
story, this author has occasion to touch most nearly
upon South Africa's most open sore—the poisoned
rift between white citizens and black—she pours
upon it, like a healing oil, the magic unction of
evangelical mysticism, so that the child and the
servant are brought into communion and rapt away
into the supra-mundane sphere for which their
innocence and the reasonless fervour kindled by a
few bizarre old phrases have fitted them.

The reader would decide for himself, wrote
Bennett, whether or not Pauline Smith has 'unusual
originality, emotional power, sense of beauty, moral
backbone'. The reader did decide, both here and
in South Africa, and her reputation was made. In

South Africa there has been a renewal of interest in her books, especially among the younger Afrikaner writers. The value of *The Little Karoo* as a link of sympathy and understanding between Dutch and English (as the two main categories of white South Africans are still called) is as great as ever. It has never been better proved than in the recorded exclamation of a Dutch, or Afrikaner, reader of this noble and gentle book: 'It is as if I had never known my own people until now!' What praise from out-siders could match that?

Imaginative writers who do not produce a stream of books get used to reproaches. If made by appreciative readers, such reproaches are far from chilling, but those who make them do not always reflect upon the many reasons that may prevent a writer from writing. The most important of these is life itself, which may impose such duties, exert such stresses, or bring such fulfilments upon a writer that it absorbs those creative energies which might have been given to art. Speculations in this place about Pauline Smith's long silence would be impertinent, but she must forgive readers of *The Little Karoo*, *The Beadle*, and *Platkops Children* if they continue to look forward hopefully to seeing her name on the title page of a new book.

June, 1949   WILLIAM PLOMER

INTRODUCTION

PAULINE SMITH was born in the Little Karoo, a name which to most people will convey nothing. Now the Little Karoo is a region of the veld in Cape Colony. It stretches east and west, high above the sea-level, immediately south of the Zwartberg Mountains. I do not know how long it is, nor does Pauline Smith, nor have I attempted to measure it out on the map; but it is very long, and very wide, and if I had been a war correspondent in the South African War, or a star reporter, I should have referred to the 'illimitable' veld. The Little Karoo is not illimitable. However, it is vast, and certainly not little save in comparison with the Great Karoo, which lies north of the Zwartberg Mountains, and with which I am not concerned.

The Little Karoo is a plain (with everywhere prospects of magnificent mountain ranges) upon which are cultivated vines, tobacco, grain, and especially ostriches, but only in rare patches—where water can be persuaded out of the earth. This water is brackish; for drinking-water the inhabitants have to depend on rain hoarded in tanks; happily there is rain, and happily the rain-water will keep sweet for six months. The inhabitants are chiefly Dutch (some of French descent), with a few English and Scots of the hardier sort. The main thing about the Little Karoo is the distances which separate the hamlets one from another; these distances are magnified by the primitive means of transport. Up to a dozen years ago the whole transport of the Little Karoo was conducted by ox-wagons, Cape-carts, donkey-wagons, mules and horses—the ox-wagon being the ship of the Karoo. Anybody who has seen an ox walk can judge the sobriety and moderation of the movement; anybody who hasn't, can't.

Cape Town, the capital of South Africa, is an important place, and I would say naught to diminish its importance; but since even today it counts barely a hundred thousand citizens, the citizens of the big towns of Britain and the United States are not likely to be over-impressed by its prestige. Nevertheless, in the eyes of the Little Karoo its prestige was and is enormous, and the inhabitants of the Little Karoo have to visit the humming, bewildering metropolis sometimes. How do they reach it? Up to as late as 1913 the favourite way for the English colonists was to trek first to Mossel Bay and then to take ship, the voyage lasting in good weather a day and a night— and in bad weather any number of days. But to get to Mossel Bay the travellers had to cross the Outeniqua Mountains, with passes of extreme steepness; the old Cradock Pass, abandoned many years ago, was so steep that the oxen would ascend the final slopes on their knees, and when the oxen could not get up even on their knees the men would take the wagons to pieces and carry them piece by piece over the summits. As for the Dutch, the South African descendants of this historic seafaring race would never trust themselves to the sea; they went to Cape Town by land, and the journey occupied days and days.

Such were the conditions in the not very distant days in which most of the Little Karoo tales are set. The colonists, as you will gather from Pauline

Smith's pictures of them, have the characteristics which you would expect from a people so situated. They are simple, astute, stern, tenacious, obstinate, unsubduable, strongly prejudiced, with the most rigid standards of conduct—from which standards the human nature in them is continually falling away, with fantastic, terrific, tragic, or quaintly comic consequences. They are very religious and very dogmatically so. They make money and save it. Lastly, they enjoy a magnificent climate, which of course intensifies their passionate love of the Karoo.

Miss Smith's father was an Englishman born in China, and her mother is a Scotswoman from Aberdeenshire. The hamlet of Oudtshoorn, on the banks of the Grobelaars and Oliphants rivers, was her birthplace. She had the advantage, from the novelist's point of view, of passing her most impressionable years amid the pristine civilization of the Little Karoo, for Oudtshoorn lay in the heart of the Little Karoo; it was then a small village, and much of its commerce was carried on by means of barter. Also the fact that her father was a doctor of medicine —the first London M.D. to settle in the Little Karoo—with a district as big as several counties, must have been an advantage to her. The doctor has contacts with the population denied to all other professions save the religious, and these contacts must exercise a powerful but indirect influence upon his children. The remoteness of Oudtshoorn may be gauged from the detail that in earlier days it had no resident minister; the communion service was only an annual event. At the period of these stories Oudtshoorn had achieved a resident minister and a quarterly communion service.

On the veld Pauline Smith was taught by gover-
nesses. At the age of twelve she migrated to England
to be educated. An early age to leave an environ-
ment, but the impressions had been made—deep,
intense, lasting. The young girl carried away with
her sufficient material for a lifetime of writing. And
since, on more than one occasion, she has refreshed
and strengthened her knowledge of Karoo life on the
spot.

Miss Smith's first literary work was done at
school—sketches of Karoo life for children; not much
prescience was needed to see that the author of these
sketches would soon be producing sketches of Karoo
life for adults. Her first published work, however,
dealt with Scottish life, and appeared in that great
organ of North Britain, *The Aberdeen Free Press.*
Thenceforward Miss Smith wrote exclusively about
the Little Karoo. Her work in periodicals received
little notice until Mr. Middleton Murry published
'The Pain' in his monthly review, *The Adelphi.*
'The Pain' was instantly greeted, from various parts
of the world, as something very fine; and I, perhaps the
earliest wondering admirer of her strange, austere,
tender, and ruthless talent, had to answer many times
the question: 'Who is Pauline Smith?' I would reply:
'She is a novelist.' 'What are her novels?' came the
inquiry. 'She hasn't written any yet,' I would say,
'but she will.' It is no part of my business here to
appraise the gifts of Pauline Smith. The reader will
decide for himself whether or not she has unusual
originality, emotional power, sense of beauty, moral
backbone.

This is her first book.

ARNOLD BENNETT

1925

THE PAIN

ALL their married, childless life of nearly fifty years Juriaan van Royen and his wife Deltje had lived in the Aangenaam valley in lands that he hired from Mijnheer van der Wenter of Vergelegen.

His lands lay an hour by foot from the Vergelegen homestead, on a little plateau on the mountain-side facing the north and the sun. The soil was poor and thin, and of all the poor men working hired lands in the Aangenaam valley Juriaan was one of the poorest. He was a tall, thin, loosely built man, slow and quiet in his speech, and slow and quiet in his movements. His lanky dust-coloured hair, fading with age instead of turning grey, and worn long like a Tak-Haar Boer's from the Transvaal, gave him a wild and unkempt look that seemed but to accentuate his gentleness of heart. For his wife Deltje his tenderness had increased with age, and, lately, with her pain. The little old woman, plump and round, with skin as soft and smooth as a child's, and a quiet, never-failing cheerfulness of spirit in spite of her pain, was dearer to him now than she had been as his bride. As his bride she had come to him up in the mountains from the harsh service of Mevrouw du Toit of Leeuw Kraal with but the clothes she wore and her Bible tied up in a red-and-white handkerchief. Mevrouw's eyes had been weak, and to save her mistress's eyes Deltje as a young girl had been taught to read. Juriaan could neither read nor write, and when on their marriage night Deltje had opened her Bible and read to him it had seemed to him that no music in all the world could be so beautiful as this. In old age her voice had become thin as a bird's, but her reading was still beautiful to him. Their years of poverty, which might have embittered them, their childlessness, which might have driven them apart, had but drawn them closer together, and it was together that they now faced Deltje's pain. And to them both, because all their lives they had been healthy, Deltje's pain was like a thing apart: a mysterious and powerful third person who, for incomprehensible reasons, clutched at Deltje's side and forced her to lie helpless for hours on the low wooden bedstead in the little bedroom.

The three-roomed mud-walled house in which the old couple lived stood close to a small stream behind a row of peach-trees. Every year from these trees they took a thankoffering of dried fruit to the Thanksgiving at Harmonie, and year by year they had beaten the stones of the peaches into the earthen floor of the living-room. Every morning Deltje sprinkled this floor with clear water from the stream and swept it with a stiff besom. The floors of the kitchen and bedroom she smeared regularly with a mixture of cow-dung and ashes called *mist*. The little house smelt always of *mist*, of strong black coffee, the beans of which were ground with peas to make it go farther, and of griddle cakes baked in the ashes of the open fire in the kitchen.

The living-room, with its three chairs strung with thongs of leather, its table scrubbed a bright yellow with the yellow-bush that grew on the mountain-side, and its gaily painted wagon-box, was a small square room with a half-door opening on to the yard behind the peach-trees. This was the only door the house possessed, for the doorways between the living-room and the kitchen and the living-room and the bed-room were empty. The partition wall, built like the outer walls of mud, did not go up to the reed-and-thatch roof, but ended, within reach, in a flat ledge on which pumpkins, twisted rolls of tobacco, little bags of seed, bars of home-made soap and water-candles, and various odds and ends were stored. From the rafters hung cobs of dried mealies, and just outside the door was the worn mealie-stamper, cut out of a tree-trunk and shaped like an hour-glass, in which the mealies were pounded into meal. There was one window, in the wall opposite the half-door. It had no glass, and was closed by an unpainted wooden shutter. Built into the wall between the living-room and the bedroom were three small shelves, and here Deltje kept their few treasures: her Bible, two cups and saucers, thick and heavy, with roses like red cabbages around them, a little pink mug, with 'A Present for a Good Girl' in letters of gold on one side of the handle and a golden Crystal Palace on the other, a green-and-red crocheted wool mat, a black-bordered funeral card in memory of Mijnheer van der Wenter's mother, an ostrich egg, and a small box lined with blue satin and covered with rows of little shells round an inch-square mirror. This was the pride of their simple hearts, and these, after fifty years of life together, were their treasures.

It was on the uppermost of the three shelves that for over a year now Deltje had kept the little bottles of 'Grandmother's Drops' which, from time to time, Juriaan had got for her from the Jew-woman's store at Harmonie, for the pain in her side. At first the drops had seemed definitely to relieve Deltje's pain, to baffle the mysterious third person who caused it, and even when the attacks became more frequent and more violent the faith of both Deltje and Juriaan had persisted because of the printed word on the wrapper. But in the month of January Juriaan's faith at last was shaken. In that month of long hot days there came a succession of attacks which exhausted all the remaining drops and left Deltje weak and helpless as an infant on the low wooden bed. And leaving her there Juriaan went down in haste to the Jew-woman's store at Harmonie.

When Juriaan reached the little white-washed store with the sign 'Winkel' printed crookedly with a blue-bag over its door, he found there Piet Deiselmann, the transport-rider between Platkops dorp and Princestown village. Piet Deiselmann, eager, impetuous, a Platkops man who was full of pride for Dutch Platkops and contempt for English Princestown, was speaking to the old Jew-woman and her grandson of the new hospital which lately had been opened in Platkops dorp, and of which Juriaan up in the mountains had never heard before. The hospital was the first to be built in the Little Karoo, and it was Dutch Platkops that had built it. In Princestown, said Piet Deiselmann contemptuously, men might still die by hundreds for want of a hospital, but in Platkops there was now no need to suffer pain. One went to the Platkops hospital so ill that one had to be carried there, and one left it leaping and praising the Lord.

All that Piet Deiselmann said of the hospital filled Juriaan, with Deltje's damp twisted face always before him, with a strange agitation of hope, wonder, and fear. For long he dared not speak. But at last, in a voice that quavered and broke, he asked:

'And must a man then be rich to go to the hospital in Platkops dorp?'

'Rich!' cried Piet Deiselmann. 'Rich? Let a man be so poor as he can be to live and at the hospital they will take him in.'

'Our Father!' said Juriaan in wonder. 'Our Father!' And it was as if, staring at the transport-rider, he already saw Deltje, her round, soft, childish face alight with joy, leaping and praising the Lord on the hospital *stoep*.

Juriaan went back to the mountains and found Deltje as he had left her on the feather bed. He poured out some drops for her, made some strong black coffee and brought it to her with a little black bread, and then sitting down on a low stool by her side spoke of the hospital in Platkops dorp. All that Piet Deiselmann had said he repeated, and in his slow quiet speech everything Piet Deiselmann had said seemed to gain a greater significance. And holding Deltje's hand in his he told her how he would put the feather bed in the ox-cart, and his reed-and-canvas tent over the cart, and his love, his heart, the joy of his life, would lie there like a bird in its nest; and so carefully as if it were the very Ark of the Lord that he were driving he would take her in to the hospital in Platkops dorp and her pain would be cured. . . . He spoke as Piet Deiselmann had done of men leaping and praising the Lord, and so great was now their faith in everything that Piet Deiselmann had said that it was as if within their old and worn bodies their hearts were already leaping and praising Him.

Early the next morning the old man began his preparations for the journey. He went first up to the kraal on the mountain-side where Jafta Nicodemus, the Vergelegen shepherd, kept his master's flocks, and it was settled that for some rolls of tobacco Jafta would take charge of his goats and his hens. His lands he must leave to God. He went back to the house, and stretching an old sail-cloth across a bamboo frame fixed this tent to his ox-cart. Under the cart he tied the big black kettle and the three-legged pot which were their only cooking utensils. He filled a small water-cask from the stream and tied that also below the cart. He brought out the painted wagon-box and fixed it in front of the cart for a seat. In the box was their small store of provisions: biltong, a small bag of coffee, a kidskin full of dried rusks, meal for griddle cakes, and the salted ribs of a goat recently killed. Behind the cart he tied some bundles of forage, and below the forage dangled a folding stool. On the floor of the cart he spread the feather bed, pillows and blankets for Deltje's nest.

When all was ready, and the two plough-oxen were inspanned, Deltje came out to the cart. She wore her black calico Sacrament gown and sunbonnet, and on her stockingless feet were *veldschoen* which Juriaan himself had made for her. She carried in her hand a red cotton handkerchief, sprinkled with white moons, in which were her Bible, the Present for a Good Girl, and the little satin-lined, shell-covered box. Excitement, or the drops, had eased for the time her pain, and her round, smooth, innocent face was alight with her faith in the Almighty, her faith in the hospital, and her faith in Juriaan. And as

6

Juriaan helped her into the cart he called her again by those tender, beautiful, and endearing names which were the natural expression of his love.

The journey to Platkops dorp by ox-cart from Vergelegen took three nights and the greater part of three days. They travelled slowly because of Deltje's pain, and with frequent outspans to rest their oxen. From Vergelegen to Harmonie all was familiar to them, but not for many years had they been farther afield than Harmonie, and even in the blazing January heat the straight grey road through the brown parched veld, with far-lying homesteads in bare parched lands, was full of interest to them. At night, when the oxen moved steadily forward with a rhythm that the darkness accented, or when they outspanned and the flames of Juriaan's fire danced to the stars above them, their hearts were filled with a quiet content. And before them, day and night, they saw not the grey stone building which Piet Deiselmann had described, but a golden wonder like the Crystal Palace on Deltje's mug. And to this golden wonder, this haven of refuge for the sick and suffering, they clung with unwavering faith through those desperate hours when Deltje, like some gentle dumb animal, lay damp and twisted in the sweat and agony of her pain.

It was towards midday on the fourth day of their journey that they reached Platkops dorp, a long straggling village on the east bank of the Ghamka river. Its low, whitewashed thatched houses stood back from the wide Hoeg Straat in gardens or green lands sloping down to the river. The street was lined with poplars, willows, and giant eucalyptus-trees,

7

and one looked up this green avenue to the Zwartkops Mountains or down it to the Teniquotas. North, south, east, and west the Platkops plain was bounded by mountain ranges, and the village lay in the heart of the plain. The hospital was the only building on the west bank of the river, and was one of the few houses built of stone. It had as yet no trees, no garden, and no green lands around it, but stood, grey and new, with even its yard unenclosed, in the open veld. It did not look in the least like the Crystal Palace on Deltje's mug, but faith, hope, and the tears which dimmed their eyes as they came within sight of it made that bare building, surrounded by a wide *stoep*, beautiful to the old couple. They crossed the river by the nearest drift and drove slowly across the veld towards it.

When Juriaan and Deltje reached the hospital steps the building was already closed and shuttered for the midday heat, and beyond the creaking of the ox-cart, and the slow 'Our Father! Our Father!' breathed by the old man as he gazed around him, all was silence. The closed doors and shutters, the empty *stoep*, upon which they had expected to see men and women, cured of their pain, leaping and praising God, did not shake their faith, as the faith of others might have been shaken, in Piet Deiselmann's report. That burning midday silence was for them but the Peace of God, and with the unquestioning patience of poverty and old age they awaited in it whatever was to befall them.

It was the matron who, half an hour later, found the ox-cart at the *stoep* steps. The matron was a kindly, capable, middle-aged woman who spoke both English and Dutch. Juriaan, holding his soft, wide-brimmed hat in his hand, answered her questions humbly. He was Juriaan van Royen, seventy-five years old, working lands on Mijnheer van der Wenter's farm of Vergelegen in the Aangenaam valley, and in the cart there, in a nest that he had made for her of the feather bed and pillows, was his wife Deltje, seventy years, come to be cured of the pain in her side. . . .

The matron turned from the old man, so wild and unkempt, so humble and so gentle, to the patient suffering little old woman seated with her bundle on the feather bed. With Juriaan's help she lifted Deltje out of the cart, and together the old couple followed her up the steps to her office. Here she left them, and in that quiet darkened room they sat on a couch together like children, hand-in-hand. They did not speak, but now and then the old man, drawing his wife towards him, would whisper that she was his dove, his pearl, his rose of the mountains, and the light of his eyes.

When the matron returned she brought with her a young pleasant-faced nurse. Nurse Robert, she explained, would take Deltje to the women's ward, and here, on his afternoon round, the doctor would examine her. Juriaan, she said, must await the doctor's report, and had better drive his cart round to the side of the hospital and outspan. Afterwards he might go back to his lands in the Aangenaam valley, or across the river to his friends in Platkops dorp. . . . It was now that for the first time the old couple realized that the hospital was to part them, and that Deltje's cure was not to be immediate. God knows what the little old woman thought as, clinging to the red-and-white handkerchief which held her

Bible, her mug, and her shell-covered box, she was led meekly away by the nurse; but for Juriaan it was as if the end of the world had come. Stunned and shaken, groping his way like a man suddenly blinded in paths that are strange to him, he went out into the dazzling sunshine and outspanned.

It was not until after coffee-time—but the old man had had no heart for coffee-making—that Juriaan was sent for to the matron's office, where the doctor was waiting for him. The doctor was an Englishman, and that he had settled in Dutch Platkops when he might have settled in English Princestown was a fact never forgotten by Platkops and never forgiven by Princestown. With the old man standing humbly before him he explained now, in slow careful Dutch, the nature of Deltje's pain. It was a bad pain. Such a pain in a younger woman might perhaps be cured, but for an old woman there was no cure, only a treatment that for a time might ease it. If Juriaan would leave his wife for some weeks in the hospital all that could be done for her the doctor would do, and it might be that after some weeks she would be well enough to go back again to the Aangenaam valley. It was for Juriaan himself to say whether she should stay, and it was for Juriaan to say whether, in the meantime, he would go back to his lands on the mountain-side or to his friends in Platkops dorp.

The old man thanked the doctor, and in the quiet measured speech which gave weight and dignity to all he said, answered that if it was in the hospital that the doctor could ease Deltje's pain it was in the hospital that she must stay. As for himself, he could not go back to the Aangenaam valley without his love, his life, his dear one. Nor could he go to his friends in Platkops dorp, for he had none there. He was a stranger to Platkops dorp. All his life had he lived on the mountain-side in the Aangenaam valley, and fifty years had his little dove lived with him. If it was not the will of the Lord that she should be cured of her pain, let the doctor do what he could to ease it, and let him, of his goodness and mercy, give Juriaan leave to camp out in the veld by the hospital to be near her until he could take her home. . . .

The doctor turned to the matron and said briefly: 'Let him stay. Take him to her.'

Juriaan followed the matron out of the office down a long, bare passage, which ended in a long, bare, bright room. In this room were six narrow white beds. By the side of each bed was a well-scrubbed locker, and above each bed hung a plain white card. The floor was as white as were the lockers, and this bright, bare cleanliness was all that at first the old man could grasp. Presently he saw that in three of the beds were women, wearing little white frilled caps that made them look like babies. And slowly it dawned upon him that one of these women, one of these babies, was Deltje.

At the sight of Deltje's smooth, round, innocent face set off so oddly by the little frilled cap, Juriaan forgot the strangeness of that strange room, forgot the white-capped heads in the other beds, forgot the matron standing by his side. He saw only his love, his joy, his treasure. And kneeling down by her side he drew her two brown hands into his and held them close against his breast.

That night, for the first time since their marriage, Juriaan and Deltje lay apart. For the old man there was neither rest nor sleep. For long he watched the lights in Platkops dorp twinkling across the river, and for long after those lights died out he watched the stars above him. He lay now on the feather bed in the cart, and now on the hard ground beneath it. He wandered like a ghost round the silent hospital buildings and came back to the ox-cart with a pain that brought tears to his eyes, though he could trace it to no definite part of his body whatever. He did not now cry 'Our Father! Our Father!' for help. The silence of the night, the silence of the grey stone building which held his little dove, his pearl, was still for him the silence of the Peace of God. But it was of a God withdrawn as if for ever from his reach.

For Deltje, too, the night was endless. For the first time in her life she lay, not in her shift and petticoats on a feather bed, but in a cotton nightgown on a narrow mattress. The unaccustomed freedom of her limbs made that narrow bed wide and empty as a desert to her. And when she slept, in short broken snatches between attacks of pain, it was to dream that Juriaan lay dead by her side and that she pressed against his cold body for comfort and warmth in vain. When morning came it was not the pain in Deltje's side that made life a mystery to the old couple. It was the pain in both their hearts.

Through the long, hot days, and the hot, still, moonlit nights that followed, the loneliness of the old people, and for Juriaan the sense of a God withdrawn, steadily increased. The ways of the hospital, the order and routine necessary for the running of it, remained to the end incomprehensible to them both.

For fifty years on their mountain-side in the Aangenaam valley life had been for them as simple as
were their daily needs, as humble as were their hearts.
In this new and bewildering world the kindness of
the English doctor, of the matron, and of the nurse
reached them only as the kindness of human beings
reaches the suffering of dumb animals. On neither
side was there, nor could there be, complete
understanding. The doctor and the matron might
know all that was to be known about the pain
in Deltje's side. About the pain in her heart and
in Juriaan's they knew nothing. And from the
inquisitiveness of the other patients in the ward the
little old woman shrank with a gentle timidity which
increased her isolation.

Alone among strangers in that bright, bare room
Deltje would lie, quiet and uncomplaining, thinking
of her house on the mountain-side: of the warmth
and comfort of the feather bed in the little bedroom
that smelt so pleasantly of *mist*: of the wooden shutter,
held by a leather thong, which creaked with the
lightest of mountain breezes: of the peach-stone
floor, with patches of sunlight crossing it from the
open half-door: of the peach-trees by the little stream
that never once in fifty years had failed them: of
fruit-drying for the Thanksgiving: of the Thanksgiving service in front of the church door at
Harmonie, when Juriaan, bareheaded among the
men, would smile across to her among the women:
of the journey home again and the first glimpse
that came to one down in the valley road of
the little brown-walled house perched high up
on the mountain-side by the peach-trees and the
stream. . . .

With his own hands had Juriaan built that house for her. For fifty years had the little stream quenched their thirst, and now they drank of a strange, lifeless water stored in tanks. For fifty years had they slept side by side in the little room with the friendly creaking shutter, and now they lay apart. . . . What was it that had brought them here? The pain in her side. . . . But she had now no pain in her side. All her pain was now in her heart. Every day she would insist to the nurse that she had now no pain in her side. And the nurse would laugh, jerk her head a little to one side, and say: 'Am I then a child? Wait a little, Tanta! Wait a little! It is for me to say when you have no pain in your side!' Of the pain in her heart she spoke only to Juriaan, when, in the evenings, he sat with her for half an hour. . . .

The old man had made his camp on that side of the hospital in which the women's ward lay, and from her bed Deltje could see the smoke of his fire as it rose into the still, hot, clear air. He seldom left the camp except to wander disconsolate round the hospital buildings, or out into the veld to attend to his oxen. Twice a day he sat for a little with Deltje in the ward, and in her thin, clear voice she would read to him from her Bible. But nothing that she read in that bright, bare room, smelling so strangely of disinfectants, brought comfort to his soul. His God was still withdrawn. Night and day the pain in his heart gave him no peace. He lived like a man in a trance. Once he was sent across the river to Platkops dorp. He saw there, in the windows of the shops in the Hoeg Straat, such things as he never before had seen and was never to see again, but they made no impression on his mind whatever. He passed down the Hoeg Straat as if in a dream of unbearable sadness and never revisited it.

It was the young, pleasant-faced Nurse Robert who had sent Juriaan in to Platkops dorp. To her there still remained the bright, hard self-confidence of youth, and in Juriaan and Deltje she saw only two aged innocents whose affairs it was her duty, and certainly her pleasure, to control. Her management of them, she was convinced, was for their good, and in all she did for them there was a certain brusque kindliness. It was she who answered for Deltje when the doctor made his daily round, and though even to the doctor Deltje would timidly protest that she had now no pain in her side her protests were drowned in the brisk common-sense of the nurse. It was Nurse Robert, too, who timed Juriaan's visit to his wife, and who, on occasions, shooed him out of the ward like a hen. And, humble and gentle as they were, the aged innocents were unaccustomed to any control beyond that love of God and of each other which up on the mountain-side had ruled their simple lives. This brisk, bright, personal interference bewildered them as nothing else in the hospital did. They came to resent it. They came to fear the pleasant-faced nurse as they had never before feared any other human being. She stood between them and the doctor: between them and the matron: and, by her refusal to allow that Deltje's pain was cured and her return to the Aangenaam valley possible, between them and everything that made life dear. With her brisk, bright contempt for the Aangenaam valley, and her praise for everything that Platkops, by contrast, produced, even to its rain-water, she drove them into a bewildered silence, and at last to flight.

It was the rain-water that, for the old couple, brought the pain in their hearts to its quiet and unnoticed crisis. In Platkops dorp the water in the furrows and rivers was so brackish that in marshy lands the ground had always a thin white coating of salt, and for drinking purposes rain-water was stored in iron tanks. For this water Deltje had what Nurse Robert considered an unreasonable distaste. It was in fact the gentle uncomplaining little old woman's one whimsy, and as the days passed and, though neither she nor Juriaan realized it, as her weakness increased, her mind dwelt more and more on the brown bubbling mountain stream which for fifty years had quenched her thirst. There came a day when in her weakness her talk wandered brokenly from the stream by the peach-trees to the well of Bethlehem, and from David's cry for the water of that well, to the River of Water of Life. . . . Juriaan sitting helpless by her side felt that his heart must break with its sorrow, that his body must die of the dull heavy pain that possessed it. . . . And slowly, through his suffering, his mind came to its deliberate resolve.

When Nurse Robert ordered Juriaan out of the ward that evening the old man left by the French door close to Deltje's bed. In those hot January nights this door was left open, and only the outer shutters were closed. The catch of these, Juriaan knew, could be raised from the outside with a knife. He knew also that Deltje's clothes had been folded away into the locker that stood by her bed. There was now only one other patient in the ward, an old, old woman dozing her life away at the far end of the room. And because there were at present no serious cases in the hospital no one was on duty at night. On all these things his mind worked slowly, but clearly, as he went out into the veld to look for his oxen. He found them, drove them back to the cart, fed them, and tied them to it. He lit a fire and made himself some strong, black, bitter coffee. He ate nothing. His stock of provisions, in spite of his daily meal from the hospital kitchen, was now so low for what he had in hand that he dared not lessen it. Night had now fallen, and after arranging the feather bed and pillows into a little nest, the old man lay down on the hard ground beneath the cart. Above him the sky was sprinkled with stars and the Milky Way made a broad white path across the heavens. But Juriaan did not look at the stars, and if God walked in His starry heavens His servant Juriaan did not know it. His God was still withdrawn. Sorrow was all his company. . . .

When the last of the lights had twinkled into darkness across the river the old man took off his *veldschoen* and crept cautiously round the hospital buildings. Here, too, all was silence and darkness. He returned to the cart and inspanned the oxen, placing stones before the wheels. Then he went back to the hospital, mounted the *stoep*, raised the hasp of the shutters with his knife, and slipped into the silent ward, where Deltje on her narrow bed, that wide and empty desert, lay quietly awake. The old man went up to her and said, without haste, without fear, but with an infinite tenderness:

'Look now, my little one! Look now, my dove! Have I not made again a nest in the cart for you? And are not our oxen once more inspanned? Come now, in my arms will I carry you out to the cart, and back to the Aangenaam valley we will go.'

He stooped down, opened the locker, and drew out her clothes. With a strange, gentle deliberation he helped her into her petticoats, and tied up her Bible, her mug, and her shell-covered box. The bottle of medicine left standing on the locker he slipped into his pocket. Then he gathered the little old woman up into his arms and carried her out into the moonlit night.

In her little nest in the feather bed Deltje lay content. She had ceased now to tremble, and not for one moment did she question Juriaan's right to act as he was doing. Already her heart was filled with that sense of security which his mere presence brought her. Already the hospital was but a dream that only for a moment had parted them. The pain in her heart had gone. Of the pain in her side she would not think. Had she not learned in the hospital how to hide it? Up in the mountains sitting by the stream and drinking of its clear brown water she would have no pain. . . . Lying through the night by Juriaan's side she would have no pain. . . . She lay back among the pillows, a gentle, dying woman, her heart overflowing with its quiet content.

Seated on the wagon-box before her Juriaan drove steadily across the veld, through the drift, and out on to the Platkops-Princestown road. Slowly his numbed heart regained its warmth. Slowly he came to feel that his God was no longer withdrawn. Here, in the ox-cart with his little love, was his God. Had He not eased her pain? If she was weak had He not given His servant Juriaan arms that were strong to carry her? Against his breast like a little child he would carry her, and so should she rest. . . .

They reached the top of the Groot Kop, the highest of the low, flat-topped hills that surrounded Platkops dorp, and here the old man wheeled round the cart and halted to rest his oxen. Below them, in the clear pale moonlight, lay the quiet village, but it was across the river that they looked, at the grey stone building standing there alone. A moment only they halted, then turned, and went on.

THE SCHOOLMASTER

BECAUSE of a weakness of the chest which my grandmother thought that she alone could cure, I went often, as a young girl, to my grandparent's farm of Nooitgedacht in the Ghamka valley. At Nooitgedacht, where my grandparents lived together for more than forty years, my grandmother had always young people about her—young boys and girls, and little children who clung to her skirts or were tossed up into the air and caught again by my grandfather. There was not one of their children or their grandchildren that did not love grandfather and grandmother Delport, and when aunt Betje died it seemed but right to us all that her orphans, little Neeltje and Frikkie and Hans, Koos and Martinus and Piet, should come to Nooitgedacht to live. My grandmother was then about sixty years old. She was a big stout woman, but as is sometimes the way with women who are stout, she moved very easily and lightly upon her feet. I had seen once a ship come sailing into Zandtbaai harbour, and grandmother walking, in her full wide skirts with Aunt Betje's children bobbing like little boats around her, would make me often think of it. This big, wise, and gentle woman, with love in her heart for all the world, saw in everything that befell us the will of the Lord. And when, three weeks after Aunt Betje's children had come to us, there came one night, from God knows where, a stranger asking for shelter out of the storm, my grandmother knew that the Lord had sent him.

The stranger, who, when my grandmother brought him into the living-room, gave the name of Jan Boetje, was a small dark man with a little pointed beard that looked as if it did not yet belong to him. His cheeks were thin and white, and so also were his hands. He seldom raised his eyes except when he spoke, and when he did so it was as if I saw before me the Widow of Nain's son, risen from the dead, out of my grandmother's Bible. Yes, as if from the dead did Jan Boetje come to us that night, and yet it was food that I thought of at once. And quickly I ran and made coffee and put it before him.

When Jan Boetje had eaten and drunk my grandparents knew all that they were ever to know about him. He was a Hollander, and had but lately come to South Africa. He had neither relative nor friend in the colony. And he was on his way up-country on foot to the goldfields.

For a little while after Jan Boetje spoke of the goldfields my grandmother sat in silence. But presently she said:

'Mijnheer! I that am old have never yet seen a happy man that went digging for gold, or a man that was happy when he had found it. Surely it is sin and sorrow that drives men to it, and sin and sorrow that comes to them from it. Look now! Stay with us here on the farm, teaching school to my grandchildren, the orphans of my daughter Lijsbeth, and it may be that so you will find peace.'

Jan Boetje answered her: 'If Mevrouw is right, and sin and sorrow have driven me to her country for gold, am I a man to be trusted with her grandchildren?'

My grandmother cried, in her soft clear voice that

was so full of love and pity: 'Is there a sin that cannot be forgiven? And a sorrow that cannot be shared?'

Jan Boetje answered: 'My sorrow I cannot share. And my sin I myself can never forgive.'

And again my grandmother said: 'Mijnheer! What lies in a man's heart is known only to God and himself. Do now as seems right to you, but surely if you will stay with us I will trust my grandchildren to you and know that the Lord has sent you.'

For a long, long time, as it seemed to me, Jan Boetje sat before us and said no word. I could not breathe, and yet it was as if all the world must hear my breathing. Aunt Betje's children were long ago in bed, and only my grandparents and I sat there beside him. Long, long we waited. And when at last Jan Boetje said: 'I will stay', it was as if he had heard how I cried to the Lord to help him.

So it was that Jan Boetje stayed with us on the farm and taught school to Aunt Betje's children. His schoolroom was the old wagon-house (grandfather had long ago built a new one), and here my grandmother and I put a table and stools for Jan Boetje and his scholars. The wagon-house had no window, and to get light Jan Boetje and the children sat close to the open half-door. From the door one looked out to the orange grove, where all my grandmother's children and many of her grandchildren also had been christened. Beyond and above the orange-trees rose the peaks of the great Zwartkops mountains, so black in summer, and so white when snow lay upon them in winter. Through the mountains, far to the head of the valley, ran the Ghamka pass by which men travelled up-country when they went looking for gold. The Ghamka river came down through this pass and watered all the farms in the valley. Coming down from the mountains to Nooitgedacht men crossed it by the Rooikranz drift.

Inside the wagon-house my grandfather stored his great brandy casks and his tobacco, his pumpkins and his mealies, his ploughs and his spades, his whips and his harness, and all such things as are needed at times about a farm. From the beams of the loft also there hung the great hides that he used for his harness and his *veldschoen*. Jan Boetje's schoolroom smelt always of tobacco and brandy and hides, and when the mud floor, close by the door, was freshly smeared with *mist* it smelt of bullock's blood and cow dung as well.

We had, when Jan Boetje came to us, no books on the farm but our Bibles and such old lesson books as my aunts and uncles had thought not good enough to take away with them when they married. Aunt Betje's children had the Bible for their reading-book, and one of my grandfather's hides for a blackboard. On this hide, with blue clay from the river bed, Jan Boetje taught the little ones their letters and the bigger ones their sums. Geography also he taught them, but it· was such a geography as had never before been taught in the Platkops district. Yes, surely the world could never be so wonderful and strange as Jan Boetje made it to us (for I also went to his geography class) in my grandfather's wagon-house. And always when he spoke of the cities and the wonders that he had seen I would think how bitter must be the sorrow, and how great the sin, that had driven him from them to us. And when, as it sometimes happened, he would ask me afterwards: 'What shall we take for our reading lesson, Engela?' I would choose the fourteenth chapter of Chronicles or the eighth chapter of Kings.

Jan Boetje asked me one day: 'What makes you choose the Prayer in the Temple, Engela?'

And I, that did not know how close to love had come my pity, answered him: 'Because, Mijnheer, King Solomon who cries, "Hear thou in heaven thy dwelling-place, and when thou hearest forgive", prays also for the stranger from a far country.'

From that day Jan Boetje, who was kind and gentle with his scholars, was kind and gentle also with me. Many times now I found his eyes resting upon me, and when sometimes he came and sat quietly by my side as I sewed there would come a wild beating at my heart that was joy and pain together. Except to his scholars he had spoken to no one on the farm unless he first were spoken to. But now he spoke also to me, and when I went out in the veld with little Neeltje and her brothers, looking for all such things as are so wonderful to a child, Jan Boetje would come with us. And it was now that I taught Jan Boetje which berries he might eat and which would surely kill him, which leaves and bushes would cure a man of many sicknesses, and which roots and bulbs would quench his thirst. Many such simple things I taught him in the veld, and many, many times afterwards I thanked God that I had done so. Yes, all that my love was ever to do for Jan Boetje was but to guide him so in the wilderness.

When Jan Boetje had been with us six months and more, it came to be little Neeltje's birthday. My grandmother had made it a holiday for the children, and Jan Boetje and I were to go with them, in a stump-cart drawn by two mules, up into a little ravine that lay beyond the Rooikranz drift. It was such a clear still day as often happens in our Ghamka valley in June month, and as we drove Neeltje and her brothers sang together in high sweet voices that made me think of the angels of God. Because of the weakness of my chest I myself could never sing, and yet that day, with Jan Boetje sitting quietly by my side, it was as if my heart were so full of song that he must surely hear it. Yes, I that am now so old, so old, was never again to feel such joy as swept through my soul and body then.

When we had driven about fifteen minutes from the farm we came to the Rooikranz drift. There had been but little rain and snow in the mountains that winter, and in the wide bed of the river there was then but one small stream. The banks of the river here are steep, and on the far side are the great red rocks that give the drift its name. Here the wild bees make their honey, and the white wild geese have their home. And that day how beautiful in the still clear air were the great red rocks against the blue sky, and how beautiful against the rocks were the white wings of the wild geese.

When we had crossed the little stream Jan Boetje stopped the cart and Neeltje and her brothers climbed out of it and ran across the river-bed shouting and clapping their hands to send the wild geese flying out from the rocks above them. Only I was left with Jan Boetje, and now when he whipped up the mules they would not move. Jan Boetje stood up in the cart and slashed at them, and they backed towards the stream. Jan Boetje jumped from the cart, and with the stick end of his whip struck the mules over the eyes, and his face, that had grown so dear to me, was suddenly strange and terrible to see. I cried to him: 'Jan Boetje! Jan Boetje!' but the weakness of my chest was upon me and I could make no sound. I rose in the cart to climb out of it, and as I rose Jan Boetje had a knife in his hand and dug it into the eyes of the mules to blind them. Sharp above the laughter of the children and the cries of the wild geese there came a terrible scream, and I fell from the cart on to the soft grey sand of the river bed. When I rose again the mules were far down the stream, with the cart bumping and splintering behind them, and Jan Boetje after them. And so quickly had his madness come upon him that still the children laughed and clapped their hands, and still the wild geese flew among the great red rocks above us.

God knows how it was that I gathered the children together and, sending the bigger boys in haste back to the farm, came on myself with Neeltje and the little ones. My grandfather rode out to meet us. I told him what I could, but it was little that I could say, and he rode on down the river. When we came to the farm the children ran up to the house to my grandmother, but I myself went alone to the wagon-house. I opened the door and closed it after me again, and crept in the dark to Jan Boetje's chair. Long, long I sat there, with my head on my arms on his table, and it was as if in all the world there was nothing but a sorrow that must break my heart, and a darkness that smelt of tobacco and brandy and hides. Long, long I sat, and when at last my grandmother found me, 'My little Engela,' she said. 'The light of my heart! My treasure!'

The mules that Jan Boetje had blinded were found and shot by my grandfather, and for long the splinters of the cart lay scattered down the bed of the river. Jan Boetje himself my grandfather could not find, though he sent men through all the valley looking for him. And after many days it was thought that Jan Boetje had gone up-country through the pass at night. I was now for a time so ill that my father came down from his farm in Beaufort district to see me. He would have taken me back with him but in my weakness I cried to grandmother to keep me. And my father, to whom everything that my grandmother did was right, once again left me to her.

My father had not been many days gone when old Franz Langermann came to my grandparents with news of Jan Boetje. Franz Langermann lived at the toll-house at the entrance to the pass through the mountains, and here Jan Boetje had come to him asking if he would sell him an old hand-cart that stood by the toll-gate. The hand-cart was a heavy clumsy one that the roadmen repairing the road through the pass had left behind them. Franz Langermann had asked Jan Boetje what he would do with such a cart? And Jan Boetje had answered: 'I that have killed mules must now work like a mule if I would live.' And he had said to Franz Langermann: 'Go to the farm of Nooitgedacht and say to Mevrouw Delport that all that is in the little tin box in my room is now hers in payment of the mules. But there is enough also to pay for the hand-cart if Mevrouw will but give you what is just.'

My grandmother asked Franz Langermann: 'But what is it then that Jan Boetje can do with a hand-cart?'

And Franz Langermann answered: 'Look now, Mevrouw! Through the country dragging the hand-cart like a mule he will go, gathering such things as he can find and afterwards selling them again that he may live. Look! Already out of a strap that I gave him Jan Boetje has made for himself his harness.'

My grandmother went to Jan Boetje's room and found the box as Franz Langermann had said. There was money in it enough to pay for the mules and the hand-cart, but there was nothing else. My grandmother took the box out to Franz Langermann and said:

'Take now the box as it is, and let Mijnheer give you himself what is just, but surely I will not take payment for the mules. Is it not seven months now that Jan Boetje has taught school to my grandchildren? God help Jan Boetje, and may he go in peace.'

But Franz Langermann would not take the box. 'Look now, Mevrouw,' he said, 'I swore to Jan Boetje that only for the hand-cart would I take the money, and all the rest would I leave.'

My grandmother put the box back in Jan Boetje's room, and gave to Franz Langermann instead such things as a man takes on a journey—biltong, and rusks and meal, and a little kidskin full of dried fruits. As much as Franz Langermann could carry she gave him. But I, that would have given Jan Boetje all the world, in all the world had nothing that I might give. Only when Franz Langermann had left the house and crossed the yard did I run after him with my little Bible and cry:

'Franz Langermann! Franz Langermann! Say

to Jan Boetje to come again to Nooitgedacht! Say to him that so long as I live I will wait!'

Yes, I said that. God knows what meaning my message had for me, or what meaning it ever had for Jan Boetje, but it was as if I must die if I could not send it.

That night my grandmother came, late in the night, to the room where I lay awake. She drew me into her arms and held me there, and out of the darkness I cried:

'Grandmother! Grandmother! Is love then such sorrow?'

And still I can hear the low clear voice that answered so strangely: 'A joy and a sorrow—a help and a hindrance—love comes at the last to be but what one makes it.'

It was the next day that my grandmother asked me to teach school for her in Jan Boetje's place. At first, because always the weakness of my chest had kept me timid, I did not think she could mean it. But she did mean it. And suddenly I knew that for Jan Boetje's sake I had strength to do it. And I called the children together and went down to the wagon-house and taught them.

All through the spring and summer months that year, getting books from the pastor in Platkops dorp to help me, I taught school for my grandmother. And because it was easy for me to love little children and to be patient with them, and because it was for Jan Boetje's sake that I did it, I came at last to forget the weakness of my chest and to make a good teacher. And day after day as I sat in his chair in the wagon-house I would think of Jan Boetje dragging his hand-cart across the veld. And day after day I would thank God that I had taught him which berries he might eat, and which bulbs would quench his thirst. Yes, in such poor and simple things as this had my love to find its comfort.

That year winter came early in the Ghamka valley, and there came a day in May month when the first fall of snow brought the river down in flood from the mountains. My grandfather took the children down to the drift to see it. I did not go, but sat working alone with my books in the wagon-house. And always on that day when I looked up through the open half-door, and saw, far above the orange grove, the peaks of the Zwartkops mountains so pure and white against the blue sky, there came a strange sad happiness about my heart, and it was as if I knew that Jan Boetje had at last found peace and were on his way to tell me so. Long, long I thought of him that day in the wagon-house, and when there came a heavy tramping of feet and a murmur of voices across the yard I paid no heed. And presently the voices died down, and my grandmother stood alone before me, with her eyes full of tears and in her hand a little damp and swollen book that I knew for the Bible I had sent to Jan Boetje. . . . Down in the drift they had found his body—his harness still across his chest, the pole of his cart still in his hand.

That night I went alone to the room where Jan Boetje lay and drew back the sheet that covered him.

Across his chest, where the strap of his harness had rubbed it, the skin was hard and rough as leather. I knelt down by his side, and pressed my head against his breast. And through my heart there ran in farewell such foolish, tender words as my grandmother used to me—'My joy and my sorrow. . . . The light of my heart, and my treasure.'

THE MILLER

Andries Lombard, the miller in the mountains at Mijnheer van der Merwe's farm of Harmonie, was a stupid kindly man whom illness had turned into a morose and bitter one. He was a tall gaunt Dutchman from the Malgas district, with black hair, black eyes, and a thick square black beard. Round his neck he wore an eelskin which his wife Mintje had tramped sixteen miles down the Aangenaam valley to borrow from old Tan' Betje Ferreira of Vetkuil. The eelskin had cured many coughs in Tan' Betje's family, but God knows how it was, though Andries wore it day and night it did not cure him of spitting blood. And in the month of September, when, in the Aangenaam valley, other men planted their lands with sweet potatoes and pumpkins and mealies, the miller said to his wife:

'I will not plant my lands. If I plant me now my lands surely by the time it comes for me to dig my potatoes and gather me my mealies I shall be dead of this cough that I have from the dust in the mill. And so surely as I am dead, the day that I am buried they will drive you out of this house in the rocks and to the man that comes after me they will give my potatoes and mealies. So I will not plant my lands. God help you, Mintje, when I am dead and they drive our children and you out in the veld the day that I am buried, but I will not plant my lands for the man that comes after me.'

All this Andries had said on a cold, clear, spring morning, sitting out in front of the mill coughing in the sun. He did not, in fact, believe that his master, a just and generous man who even now sent help up to the mill when work there was heavy, would drive Mintje and her children like beasts out in the veld when he died, but it gave him a strange malicious pleasure to say it and to make Mintje believe it. Mintje was a timid, humble woman who loved her husband and ran to serve him with quick fluttering movements like those of a frightened hen. But, unlike a hen, she ran always in silence, and it was the new cunning of his illness which had taught Andries how to make her suffer in this silence. If God, Who loved him, made the miller suffer, he, who loved Mintje, would make Mintje suffer. So it was that Andries reasoned, and through all his blundering cruelty, and through the wild and bitter exultation with which her tears and the quick rise and fall of her bosom filled him, there ran the memory of his old affection for her and the yearning for her love.

Through the spring and summer months, while his lands lay desolate on the mountain-side, the miller's illness rapidly increased. He made no effort to control the sudden bursts of fury which more and more frequently possessed him, and which drove his children from him in terror. He delighted in their terror as he delighted in Mintje's tears. Yet invariably after these storms his heart was tormented by a remorseful tenderness for which he could find no expression. There were days when Andries, having driven Mintje away from him, would have given all the world to call her back again to speak with her of his sorrow and his love. He never spoke of either. It was to make Mintje suffer that, in the autumn, when other men gathered their harvests, he dug for himself a grave in a corner of his empty lands. It was to make her suffer again that, in the month of May, when the pastor of Platkops came on his yearly visit to the Aangenaam valley, Andries refused, for the first time since their marriage, to go with his wife to the Thanksgiving at Harmonie.

'Why then should I go?' he cried. 'Is there a thing this day in my lands but the grave that I have dug there? Is it for my grave that you would have me praise the Lord? Go you, then, if you will, and praise him for it, Mintje, but surely I will not.'

So it was that on the Thanksgiving morning Andries sat alone in front of the mill while Mintje and his children went down the mountain-side to Harmonie. The square whitewashed church, built by Mijnheer van der Merwe for the Aangenaam valley, stood at a little distance from the homestead, close to a poplar grove near the Aangenaam river. Round about it went four straight white paths made of the stones which Mijnheer van der Merwe's sons had dug out of the mountain-side for gold. They had found no gold, and the old man had cried:

'It is well, my children! The judgments of the Lord are more to be desired than gold, yea, than much fine gold.' And round his white church he had put their white stones as a sign to his sons from the Lord.

It was to these straight white paths that, on the Thanksgiving morning, the men of the Aangenaam valley brought their gifts of pumpkins and mealies, dried fruit, corn, goats, pigs and poultry. On a long trestle-table in front of the church door the women spread their offerings of baked meats and pastries, their konfijts and waffels and custards and cakes. Every year, for eleven years, Mintje had taken *must*-rusks to the table, and Andries had taken pumpkins and mealies to the paths. This year the miller had nothing to give and no wish to give. But, when he drove her from him, Mintje carried as always her offering of rusks tied up in a spotless white cloth.

For a little while after Mintje left him Andries sat brooding in front of the mill. Mintje had left him in tears, but today her tears had brought him no pleasure. There was a pain in his chest, in his heart, and a strange humming lightness in his head. The morning air was sharp and clear, and in it the voices of his children came back to him shrill and sweet as they scrambled like conies among the rocks. Mintje's voice he did not hear, and suddenly it was the one sound in all the world that he wished to hear. If Mintje would but turn and call to him: 'Andries! Andries!' he would go to her, and this pain in his chest, this lightness in his head would surely leave him. . . . But Mintje did not call. She did not even dare to turn and look back. Timid, humble, down the mountain-side she went, in little quick fluttering runs, to thank the Lord through her tears for His many mercies.

Down in the valley at Harmonie carts and wagons were now being outspanned, and close to the low mud wall of the church-land a fire had been lighted for coffee-making. From his plank seat in front of the mill Andries could see the smoke of this fire rising straight up into the clear blue sky like a burnt-offering to the Lord. In the poplar grove the winter sunshine turned the tall yellowing trees into spires of gold. Through Mevrouw van der Merwe's flower garden, and through the grove, ran the brown bubbling stream which up here in the mountains turned the mill wheel. The stream joined the Aangenaam river close to the little whitewashed store where the old Russian Jew-woman, Esther Sokolowsky, kept shop with her grandson Elijah. Every year the Jew-woman, who went by no other name in the valley, baked a cake for the Thanksgiving.

Andries, looking down now on the store, remembered how, for the first Thanksgiving after she came to Harmonie, the Jew-woman, old and bent and thin, cringing like a hunted animal, with her thin grey hair tied up in a handkerchief, had come to Mevrouw van der Merwe with a cake on a blue-and-white plate. Standing on the *stoep*, where Andries was waiting for Mijnheer, the Jew-woman had said to Mevrouw:

'If it is not right for Mevrouw to take this cake that I have made, to sell it at the Thanksgiving for the Lord, let Mevrouw give it to her grandchildren, for it is a good cake that I have made for a thank-offering for my grandson and me.'

And Mevrouw had answered: 'Is not your Lord also my Lord?' And had herself carried the cake down to the table before the church door.

Every year round her cake the Jew-woman put a little frill of coloured paper, and when one opened this frill and held it up to the light one saw in it the little trees and houses, and the little strange animals which she had cut there. The paper frill had always been a source of wonder to the miller and his children, but for the old Jewess herself Andries had a pity that was not unmixed with fear. Terrible things had happened to the Jew-woman in her own country before she had escaped from it with her grandson Elijah. It was the memory of these things that made her creep about her house like a frightened animal. In no other human being had Andries ever seen such fear as one saw sometimes in the Jew-woman's eyes. . . . And now suddenly, as he sat in front of his mill on this Thanksgiving morning, it was not the Jew-woman's eyes that he saw before him, but his wife, Mintje's, terror-stricken through her tears.

In an agony that was half physical, half mental, the miller rose from his seat. God forgive him, he thought in horror, but if it was the terrible things that had happened to her in her own country that had turned the Jew-woman into a frightened animal, it was he, Andries, who had turned Mintje into a nervous hen. . . . Mintje had not been a hen when he married her. When he married her she had been his little dove. Yes, like a little bird had she come fluttering into his arms on the day that he asked her to be his wife. . . . He could feel now the pressure of her dark brown head against his breast. He could hear now the first, shy, half-whispered 'Andries! Andries!' of her wonder and her love. . . . God forgive him the evil he had done, but never again would he drive Mintje from him in tears. If he could but reach her now, to speak with her of his sorrow, this pain in his chest, this lightness in his head would surely go and she would be again his little dove, his little gentle fluttering bird, soft and warm against his breast.

Weak and shaken by emotion and pain the miller had already crossed the mill yard and was now making his way uncertainly down the mountain-side. Down in the valley they were ringing the old slave bell, which was now the church bell, and in the church-land men, women and children were gathering together for the opening psalm. Somewhere among them was Mintje, and now come what might of it, to Mintje the miller must go. As a worshipper to the Thanksgiving he would not and could not go. He had nothing to do with the Thanksgiving. Did not all the valley know that he had not planted his lands? Did not all the valley know that there was nothing this day in his lands but the grave that he had dug there? Could a man come so with empty hands to the Lord? It was not to the Lord that he was going now, but to Mintje. It was not the Lord who could ease his pain of body and mind. It was Mintje.

When he reached the quiet, deserted homestead the miller slipped into Mevrouw van der Merwe's flower garden, and through it into the poplar grove. If he could get close to the mud wall of the church-land he might perhaps be able to call to Mintje when she came, as was her custom, to help with the coffee-making at the fire. In the grove, cut off from the brilliant winter sunshine, the air was bitterly cold, and his body, which pain and exertion had thrown into a heavy sweat, grew suddenly chilled. Pushing his way through the undergrowth, coughing feebly, he came at last to a slight clearing from which he could see the gathering in the church-land. And here, leaning up against a tree trunk, he halted.

In the church-land, facing the church door, the old, white-haired pastor of Platkops was addressing his people. On one side of him, bareheaded, stood the men and boys of the Aangenaam valley. On the other, the women and girls. In a group apart were the native servants, and behind the table stood Mevrouw van der Merwe and her daughters, with Classina October, the Kaffir girl, waving a cow-tail before them. Close to the table, among the women stood Mintje, holding her little Andrina by the hand. The year had been a good one, and looking now from group to group it seemed to Andries that he alone, in all the valley, was not at the Thanksgiving. He and the Jew-woman, who though she baked a cake for the table, and came every year to look over the wall, remained always, by her faith, an outcast from the gathering.

Of what the pastor said Andries at first heard little. The humming in his ears was now intense, and added to it there was a new, suffocating pressure in his throat. Only for a moment, as the Jew-woman, creeping towards him, threw him into a sudden panic, did this pressure lessen, and in that moment he heard, with a curious, thin, almost painful distinctness, the pastor cry:

'Is it by gifts alone that a man shall be judged? Surely not, my children! So many men as there are in the world, so many ways there are to praise the Lord, and who can tell how another serves Him? Look, my little ones! The sacrifices of God are a broken spirit: a broken and a contrite heart He will not despise, for He Himself has said it. . . .'

As suddenly as it had lifted the pressure in his ears, in his throat, descended upon him again, and the miller turned, wild-eyed and suffering, to the old Jewess for help. He tried to ask her to call Mintje to him, but he could not speak. Nor could he hear what it was that the Jew-woman, looking at him so strangely, said. For some reason which he could not understand she took him by the hand and began leading him away from the wall, through the grove, towards her store. The lightness in his head had gone now to his legs, and though his heart was still crying out for Mintje, his legs, which he could not control, were taking him away from her. He tried to explain this to the Jew-woman, but he could explain nothing, and in a vain effort to gain relief he put his hand up to his throat and tore the eelskin from his neck. He stumbled, and as he stumbled blood rushed from his mouth soaking his beard, his shirt, his coat sleeves. The Jew-woman drew him down on to a low mound among a little heap of rustling yellow leaves, and leaving him there, ran, unbuttoning her apron as she went, down to the stream. She dipped her apron into the clear running water and brought it back to press, icy cold, against his throat and chest. She took off her shawl and made a pillow for his head. She took off her handkerchief, letting her thin grey hair fall about her shoulders, and soaking the handkerchief held it to his lips. To and from the stream she ran till Andries, in an agony that at last gave him speech, cried:

'But Mintje! Mintje!' and struggling to rise fell back fainting among the yellow leaves.

For a moment the old Jewess hesitated, then ran, back through the undergrowth, towards the churchland. Here, in the brilliant sunshine, men, women and children were singing together: 'Praise God, ye servants of the Lord.' They were still singing when Mintje, kneeling down by his side, drew the miller up into her arms and cried through her tears:

'Andries! Andries!'

The miller opened his eyes and saw above him the
little dove, the little gentle fluttering bird to whom
his love and sorrow were never now to be spoken.
With a vague, weak movement he raised his arm and
tried to draw Mintje's head down on to his blood-
stained breast. He failed, slipped from her grasp
into the rustling yellow leaves, and lay still.

THE SINNER

Niklaas Dampers, the bijwoner* who worked
Mijnheer van Reenen's lands near Platkops dorp,
was fifty-six years old when his favourite daughter,
Saartje, married and went to live with her husband in
the Philip district. Niklaas had prayed that Saartje
might never leave him, and the Lord's strange
answer to his prayer filled his mind with an un-
reasoning hatred of his ten remaining children and
of his wife Toontje. The bijwoner was a small, weak,
religious man, with pale red-lidded eyes, arms that
seemed too long for his body, and a heart that was
full of bitterness and the fear of the Lord. Of all his
children, it seemed to him now, Saartje alone had been
dear to him, and if he had ever loved his wife he had
long ago forgotten it. Toontje was a tall, patient,
silent woman, who shared with none the secrets of
her soul. God might know what Toontje hid in her
heart, but in all their years of poverty together
Niklaas had never fathomed it, and now that
Saartje had left him his wife's patience and silence,
and his own increasing hatred of her, became a
torture which drove the bijwoner to the verge of
madness. And it did drive him to Koba Nooi for
comfort.

Jacoba Nooi, a stranger to the district, had but
lately come to Platkops dorp on a visit to her uncle,
the bijwoner Godlieb Nooi, whose lands came next
to those of Niklaas Dampers. Koba was a plump

* Bijwoner=by-dweller: a man who lives on the farm of
another working certain lands in part-shares for the owner.

unmarried woman of forty, with a round childish face, a tongue like a running sluice, and a gentle sing-song voice. On Sundays, with an air of great simplicity and innocence, she wore a sprigged cotton gown and a hat trimmed with ribbons. All other women of her age in the bijwoning class wore plain black dresses and black calico sunbonnets, and Koba's hat made much talk among them. So also did her hand-mirror, which was rimmed with little shells and set with larger shells at the back. Such a mirror had never before been seen by any bijwoner's wife or daughter in the Platkops district. Many strange things were whispered about it, and many more about Koba herself, who, when her work was done, would sit out in the yard, or down by the river, flashing her mirror in the sun.

Of the mirror, and of the whispers about Koba, Niklaas knew nothing. Toontje had never spoken of them to him, and his own distress of mind was now so great that he himself spoke to none whom he might avoid. For many years this weak, harsh, embittered man had feared the Lord and worshipped Him. For many years he had believed that at the last the Lord would deal justly with such righteousness as his, and visit vengeance upon all such sinners as were most other men in the Platkops district. Through all his years of poverty this alone had been his comfort. And now because Saartje had loved a stranger from the Philip district and left her parents to marry him, neither righteousness nor sin, neither justice nor vengeance, had any meaning for the bijwoner and he searched for his God in vain.

Towards the end of February month, by Mijnheer van Reenen's orders, Niklaas had begun to cut his tobacco, and it was now hanging in open shelters on the land to dry. Andries van Reenen was a hard master, whose one passion, even now when men said that he was dying, was the tobacco he grew on his various lands throughout the Platkops district. Any bijwoner who did not plant, weed, cut, dry, strip, dip, and twist to please him he dismissed without pity, and all men knew it. Niklaas, a good servant, was never, in the tobacco season, without fear of this dismissal. This year the crop had been good, and his master, for the moment, was satisfied. But in a few weeks now the tobacco would be dry, and then, waiting for a dewy night to soften the leaves, the bijwoner must take the stalks from the shelters and begin to 'strip'. If a man stripped the leaves from the stalks in weather that was too dry, the leaves crumbled and would not afterwards 'twist'. If he stripped them in weather that was too damp they mildewed. A dewy night he must wait for if the wrath of Mijnheer were not to overtake him.

All this Niklaas knew, but it was not of this that he thought as he walked across the hot, empty lands, from shelter to shelter, one still March day. Mijnheer van Reenen might be merciless to his bijwoners if they failed with his tobacco, but no man, it seemed to Niklaas now, could be so merciless to another as God had been to him in taking Saartje to Philip dorp and leaving Toontje in Platkops. If the Lord now, by some miracle, had taken Toontje to Philip and left Saartje in Platkops how gladly would he have praised Him! But God was no longer his friend.

God was, in fact, but another Toontje . . . as patient and as secret, and as silent.

This thought brought the bijwoner to the bank of the river. And as he stood there with his soul in a torment of hatred that now embraced both his wife and the Almighty, Koba Nooi, with a little giggle from down below him, flashed her mirror up on to his face, on to his shirt sleeve, on to the bushes and stones that lay between them, and drew him slowly, slowly, down the bank towards her.

The bijwoner could never afterwards remember how he reached the river-bed, but presently he found himself seated by Koba's side with the mirror in his hands. Niklaas, who had never seen the sea, held the mirror-back towards him, and drew his fingers gently over the smooth round shells. Koba, who had been to Zandtbaai, and seen not only the sea but the ships that sail upon it, told him, in her gentle sing-song voice, many strange and wonderful things about it. Then suddenly, with a little giggle, she twisted the mirror round, and Niklaas saw before him part of his own wild and sorrowful face, and part of Koba Nooi's plump, round, childish one pressing against it. Giggling still, Koba twisted the mirror back, then round again, then back and round and round till Niklaas, who saw his face only on Sundays, in a small cracked piece of looking-glass that Toontje kept in a drawer, was like a drunken man in his bewilderment. And because his heart was empty now of all sense of righteousness and sin, of all fear of justice and of vengeance, there swept into it a wild tumult of desire that was but another madness.

Three weeks later, while Niklaas's tobacco still

hung in its shelters, Toontje went, a calm inscrutable woman in a black calico gown and sunbonnet, to the farm of Mijnheer van Reenen, which lay an hour by foot from Platkops dorp. Here Andries van Reenen, a rich man and a hard master, respected and feared, but loved by none even among his own family, was dying slowly of stone in the bladder. Toontje's father had been one of his many bijwoners, on lands that he once had owned and afterwards sold, in the Kombuis—a valley which lay to the north of the district among the Zwartkops foothills. Not for many years had Toontje visited the farm, and not once since her marriage had she spoken with her master alone. When she came to the house the old man sat out on the *stoep* in a big iron-wood chair made specially for his comfort. His face was grey and drawn, and he answered her greeting with an abrupt, bitter 'Good day'. In her youth in the Kombuis this tall patient woman, so quiet in her speech, so controlled in all her movements, had been free and beautiful to him as a roe-buck in the mountains. But he did not now remember it and saw in her only the bearer of news about that last passion of his life, his tobacco.

'How goes it?' he asked.

'Mijnheer,' answered Toontje, 'the tobacco dries well. But look how it is! Five-and-twenty years has Niklaas worked for Mijnheer, and a good servant has he been, but now a madness has come upon him and up to the Kombuis with Koba Nooi he has gone, and is working tobacco there for the Hollander.'

'Niklaas? In the Kombuis!' cried his master, incredulous. And he added in a sudden blaze of anger, 'May his soul burn in hell and Koba's also.'

'Mijnheer,' said the bijwoner's wife in her quiet level voice, 'may God forgive him in his madness, but is it for Mijnheer and me to judge him?'

'Fool,' thundered the old man, 'are you then also mad?'

And Toontje answered: 'Mijnheer knows that once I was mad. Mijnheer knows how my madness ended. Did Mijnheer never himself go up to the Kombuis? Or is it that he has perhaps forgotten?'

'Toontje!' cried the old man, his mind moving, slow and bewildered, from his tobacco to the past. 'Toontje!'

'Andries!'

For a moment their eyes met, and in that moment the secret which Toontje hid in her heart and Niklaas had never fathomed, lay bared between them. The moment passed, and, as if it had never been, the bijwoner's wife, calm, inscrutable, said to her master:

'Mijnheer, see how it is. My son Ockert is now sixteen years, and if Mijnheer will but trust his tobacco to Ockert and me, so soon as it is dry, after the first dewy night, we will strip and afterwards do all as it should be done till Niklaas comes again from the Kombuis. Mijnheer knows that such a madness will not last, and Mijnheer knows that I will serve him well. Have I not served Mijnheer for more than Niklaas's five-and-twenty years? And what is it that I ask of him now but still to serve him?'

'And is this then all that you will have of me,' asked the old man slowly. 'You that once lived for me in the Kombuis?'

'Mijnheer, there is but one thing more. If Mijnheer will but say, to all that speak of it, that he himself has sent Niklaas up to the Kombuis, to see how the Hollander works his tobacco. . . .'

In a flash, in that passion for his tobacco which through all his months of terrible dying was still to hold him, Andries van Reenen's anger blazed up afresh.

'And to save your husband Niklaas you ask me this,' he cried. 'A fool that could leave his tobacco and you for Koba Nooi?'

'Mijnheer! Mijnheer!' answered Toontje, 'did I not marry the fool to save the master?'

Again the old man's mind went slowly back to the past. 'God forgive me that and many other things,' he said. 'Go. I will say it.'

That night Toontje made up a small bundle of clothing for Niklaas, and with great labour wrote him a letter. This letter she slipped into the bundle, but in the middle of the night she rose, withdrew the letter, and after adding a single sentence again inserted it. Next day she took the bundle up to the morning market, and finding a wagon there from the Kombuis gave it to the driver to deliver to Niklaas. And to those that stood by her she said:

'Look now! Up to the Kombuis has the master sent Niklaas, to see how the Hollander works his tobacco, and the lands by the river he has left to Ockert and me.'

Up in the Kombuis—that most beautiful and most isolated of all the valleys among the Zwartkop foot-hills—Niklaas, having abandoned his wife and his children, his lands and his tobacco, his conscience and his God, now lived in a mud-walled, one-roomed hut with Koba Nooi and worked for his new master the Hollander. The Hollander was a young and ambitious man who had built a small factory in the valley and was working tobacco there in ways that were new and strange to Niklaas. Koba's ways were also strange to him, and, as the fever of his madness subsided, it seemed to the bijwoner that this plump, pleasant, and rather greedy woman, with her gentle chatter and her little giggle, was as secret as his own wife Toontje. Toontje's silence, it dawned upon him slowly, hid no more from him than did Koba's talk, which was often now as bewildering to him as was her mirror. The mirror she kept in a little card-board box shaped like a coffin, and there came a day when Niklaas found her down by the Hollander's gaily painted house flashing her mirror in the sun. When questioned she giggled, slipped the mirror into its box, and said, in her gentle sing-song voice:

'Ach no, then, Niklaas! Leave me and my mirror alone, or I also one day will be sending your clothes after you like your wife Toontje!'

The bundle which Toontje had sent him was stowed away on top of the mud wall, under the thatch, and because of Koba's jeers Niklaas had never opened it.

This meeting, for Niklaas, was the beginning of a vague uneasiness about Koba which steadily increased as her disappearances from the hut became more and more frequent and prolonged. In the factory also the bijwoner was far from happy, and there was constant friction between him and his new master. No man in all the Kombuis valley knew more about Platkops tobacco than Niklaas had learned in his long service with Mijnheer van Reenen, but he parted with his knowledge to the Hollander in a spirit of bitter, contemptuous niggardliness which not only the young man, but Koba Nooi, resented.

One day Koba said to him strangely: 'Ach no, then, Niklaas! Did I not bring you here to please the Hollander, and now you will not please him!'

'But, Koba,' said Niklaas, 'was it only for this that we came to the Kombuis . . . . to please the Hollander?'

'Ach no, then,' answered Koba. 'Such a nice young man as the Hollander is, who would not wish to please him? Rich he is and all, and did he not need such a man as you, that knows all about Platkops tobacco, when I brought you here to help him?'

'But Koba,' began Niklaas again. . . .

'Ach no, then, Niklaas!' interrupted Koba. 'If the Hollander says to you "Go!" where will you go? To your daughter Saartje, or your wife Toontje? Say for me now, which will it be?'

Niklaas could not say, and knew that Koba knew it. That night he lay for long awake, and in the new anxiety which Koba's question had aroused, the conscience which he had so triumphantly abandoned in his flight from Platkops regained its possession of his soul. His sense of righteousness and sin returned to him, his fear of justice and of vengeance, and he who had once counted himself among the elect now knew himself to be among the damned. In the days that followed so great became his distress that he tried even to speak with Koba of their sin. But no regrets for the past, no fears for the future, had ever troubled Koba, and she would not, to oblige the weak and repentant Niklaas, allow them to trouble her now.

'Ach no, then, Niklaas,' she said, 'surely now if you talk to me so both you and your clothes after you will I send out of the Kombuis, and where then will you go?'

And Niklaas saw himself for ever a prisoner in the Kombuis, a sinner who had sold himself to Koba Nooi and the Devil.

In September month Niklaas planted out for the Hollander the tobacco which had been sown for him in April. The lands lay some distance from the factory, and here Niklaas was free from both Koba and his master, but this freedom brought no peace to his soul. His thoughts, burdened always now by the sense of his sin, went back in a dull hopeless brooding to his own lands near Platkops dorp, to his wife Toontje, for whom his hatred had long since died down, to his children, and to Saartje in the Philip district. In the lands, he thought, a stranger must now be planting out tobacco for Mijnheer van Reenen as he was here planting it out for the Hollander. But where, when his hard and pitiless old master had turned them off his lands, had Toontje gone with the children? There was but one thing she could do, he thought. And he saw his children adopted into the homes of others, as the children of poor whites were sometimes adopted, and Toontje herself in the house of strangers. So, he thought, was his sin, and their shame, published to all the world in Platkops dorp.

There came a day when Niklaas, in a drifting, aimless misery of remorse and indecision, ceased working in the lands and went down to the factory. As he neared the Hollander's gay blue wooden house he saw Koba on the steps of the *stoep*. She wore her sprigged cotton gown and her hat trimmed with ribbons, and sat there flashing her mirror in the sun. As Niklaas watched her the Hollander himself came out of the house and sat down beside her. Niklaas heard Koba's little giggle and her pleasant sing-song, 'Ach no, then, Mijnheer!' as the Hollander put his arm round her waist. For a moment he lingered. Then as Koba, pressing her face against the Hollander's, held the mirror up before them, the bijwoner turned and fled.

When he came, exhausted, to the hut, Niklaas was clear about one thing only—he was no longer Koba's prisoner. With no thought but of escape he gathered together his few possessions, adding Toontje's bundle to the rest, and left the hut. Making his way along a low line of kopjes, bright with spring flowers, he left the valley behind him and came at last, after several hours to the Platkops–Philip dorp road. Here he was brought to a sudden halt, for by that road a man must travel either south or north. And neither south to Platkops where his children were bonded like slaves, nor north to Philip dorp, where his shame would be Saartje's, could he now go. His way must lie to the east, ahead of him, among the pathless foothills by which in time he might come to the Ghamka pass and so through the mountains to the Malgas district. The Malgas district, in the Great Karoo, was dry and waterless, and no tobacco was grown there. All his life he had lived in tobacco lands, but now to Malgas he must go, and live how and where he could. . . .

He turned aside to the shelter of a prickly-pear thicket, and sat there, a weak, foolish, suffering and repentant old man, staring hopelessly with pale red-lidded eyes at the road before him. He thought again of his tobacco lands down by the river near Platkops dorp, of Toontje and his children, of Saartje, and through his soul there swept a desolation such as he had never before endured. Around him all the veld was gay as a carpet with flowers, and close to where he sat was a bright crimson cluster that made him think of the burning bush out of which the Lord had once spoken to Moses. But the Lord never now spoke to His people, and who was he, a sinner from the Kombuis, that the Lord should speak to him?

He turned from the flowers and began re-arranging his bundles for the trek to Malgas. A slip of paper fluttered out on to the ground and he stopped to pick it up. Laboriously, holding it close to his pale weak eyes, he spelled out Toontje's letter.

'Niklaas', it ran, 'the master told me this day that he will leave the lands to Ockert and me till you come again to Platkops dorp, and to all that speak of it he says that he himself has sent you to the Kombuis to see how the Hollander works his tobacco. This I will tell to our daughter Saartje, for surely, Niklaas, when your madness leaves you, you will come again to our children and me,

TOONTJE.'

And then came that sentence which Toontje had risen in the night to add: 'God forgive me, Niklaas, if I should judge you, for there is not one of us that has not sinned.'

Many, many times did Niklaas read this letter before its meaning became clear to him, and then it was as if in pity and forgiveness God Himself had spoken. With stupid, fumbling fingers, and eyes made redder than ever with tears, he tied his bundles together and took the road to Platkops dorp.

ANNA'S MARRIAGE

ANNA was the youngest of my parents' children and she was the dearest to my mother of us all. She was fair and small, like our grandmother Fourie, and gentle in her ways, and though there was not one of us that did not love her, her place was always at my mother's side. My father had no favourite among us. When I married Otto Joubert of Malgas and my father gave to me the farm of Blaukops for my portion, he did only what seemed right to him and to my brothers also. But my mother could not see this. My mother wanted me to marry, rather, rich Hans Lategan of Uitkijk, and she had had it always in her mind that Blaukops would go to my sister Anna. Because of this, and because of her love for Anna, my mother could not be just to Otto and me. On my wedding-day it was as if I could hear her cry:

'See how it is! My daughter Griet has chosen a man to please herself, but surely my little Anna will marry to please her mother.'

Yes, well I knew what was in my mother's mind when she looked at me on my wedding-day. And in my heart I answered her:

'Surely I have chosen my man to please myself! Out of all the world I have chosen him! Wait now, and see if Anna will not do so also.'

So it was between us then, and from that day my mother could not rest until my father bought the farm of Brandtwacht for my sister Anna. Anna's farm came next to mine, on the way to our brother

Ludovic's, and my father, who was now an old man, settled it so that Otto and Ludovic should work the Brandtwacht lands between them until my sister Anna married. To please my mother, also, before he died, he built for Anna there a grey stone house that stood close by the road. My mother was proud of Anna's house. From the wide stone *stoep* she would look east and look west, look north and look south, and in all the Platkops district she would see no man who was good enough for her little Aantje.

It was six months after the house was built, and three months after my father died, that Philip Coetzee, whom Otto had known up-country, came down to the Platkops district looking for gold in the Credo mountains. Much talk about gold his coming made in the district, but always when men spoke of it Otto would say to me:

'Wait now! Surely mischief and sorrow will come of it.'

He said to me also: 'See how it was in the Malgas district! If Philip Coetzee went looking for gold, presently round about him there was trouble among neighbours, and Philip would go from one to the other stirring up strife between them about their landmarks or their water-rights or whatever it might be, and driving them gently, gently, with his pleasant ways and his easy talk, to his brother Stephan, the attorney, in his office in Malgas dorp. Many times I have seen it so, and surely now this gold that he says he will find in the Credo mountains is but dust that he digs to throw in our eyes to blind us.'

Otto said that. And even as he said it Philip was

working quietly, quietly against us, buying old Jan Jafta with drink to go to my mother at Welgevonden and lie to her there that Otto led water from Anna's lands of Brandtwacht to our own lands of Blaukops. Gently, gently Philip worked it, and when at last Jan Jafta went to my mother my mother believed him.

God forgive Jan Jafta the evil that he did that day, and God forgive me also, for when Otto would have gone with brother Ludovic to reason with my mother I would not let him go. It was as if there came that day a storm in my heart that I could not make still, and to Ludovic I cried:

'Look now, Brother! Neither to Brandtwacht nor to Welgevonden shall Otto go. From this day it is finished between my mother and me. Let my mother believe this evil of Otto! What is my mother to me?'

And I said also: 'Well, my mother knows how it was between us when I married Otto. No kindness did she show me then, and if it is lies that she will listen to now, let all Platkops lie to her and against all Platkops I will stand by my husband Otto. Go, tell my mother that. It is the last that I will say to her.'

Yes, that message did I send to my mother. I could not see how like my mother's love for Anna was my own love for Otto. Strong and bitter was our love, and for many weeks there passed no sign between us. Even when Ludovic spoke of the lameness that came upon my mother now and kept her always at her own house of Welgevonden I would not turn my heart towards her. 'Look now,' I would say, 'what is my mother's lameness to me? My mother has but to sit and old Jan Jafta will lie to her.'

And then one day brother Ludovic came to the house with Otto and said: 'See now, Griet, the game that Philip Coetzee has played us! Well he knew what a Malgas man might tell of him, so first he makes mischief between our mother and Otto, so that you go no more to Welgevonden, and then he goes to the kloof that runs by the farm from the Credo mountains, looking for gold where no gold is, and makes love to our sister Anna. Old Jan Jafta himself it was that watched him. And when he saw how Anna walked through the lands to meet him he went to our mother and told her how Philip Coetzee had paid him to lie to her. Other things also he told her. And now when our mother sees the evil that is in him Anna cries to all the world that she will marry him. Even in community of property she will marry him and there is not one of us that can save her.'

When Ludovic told me this it was as if the storm that had been so long in my heart went suddenly down. I stood there, looking at him, and it was my own sin that I saw, driving Anna, who was so dear to us all, away from my mother to Philip Coetzee of Malgas. And that same hour I went to my mother at Welgevonden.

When I came to the farm that lay so beautiful at the foot of the Credo mountains, I found my mother alone in the living-room. She sat at the head of the long yellow table, and I do not know how it was, but she wore her bonnet. My mother never wore her bonnet except when she went to the dorp for Sacrament. But this day, sitting alone in her own house, with her Bible open before her, she wore it. And it was as if I knew by this that my mother's heart was breaking.

God knows what it was that I said to my mother that day, but for so long as she lived there came again no bitterness between us. A little while I sat with her there, and presently I went to my sister Anna.

Anna, whose place had been always at my mother's side, sat now alone in her own room, sewing. I said to her:

'Anna! God forgive the bitterness that has been between my mother and me, for surely I sinned in this and sorrow has come of it. But look now! My sorrow this day is as nothing to the sorrow that will come to you if you marry young Philip Coetzee of Malgas. Who is this Philip Coetzee that you should break our mother's heart to marry him? If he could lie to our mother about Otto, will he not lie also to you? Think now, my darling! All the years that he worked for him our father trusted Otto in everything that he did, and is there one of our brothers this day that trusts Philip Coetzee? I tell you, in all the Malgas district there is no man that trusts him, and all the world can see that he plays with you for the Brandtwacht lands. It is for this that he works now so hard with his love talk and his kisses. It is not kisses alone that he will give you when he marries you, my child. He will play with you then as he plays with his dog, and he will take the lands out of your hands, and when he has lost you the lands he will leave you. Did he not leave Johanna Marincowitz so when they made her father bankrupt?'

All this I said, standing in the room where Anna sat sewing. And Anna, sitting by the window, looked out across the lands and smiled to herself, and it was as if I could hear the song that she sang all day in her heart for young Philip Coetzee. I ran to her and cried:

'Anna! Anna! It will not be what you think!' And I took her into my arms and shook her, and took her into my arms again and held her there, and knew that I could not save her.

So it was that Anna married young Philip Coetzee of Malgas and went to live with him in the grey stone house that my father had built for her. Anna was proud of her house, as my mother had been, and Philip Coetzee bought much fine furniture for it in Platkops dorp. Anna was like a child about her furniture, and when he saw how it filled her mind Philip would buy now this and now that to please her. Because of her lameness my mother could never go to Brandtwacht to see Anna's things. She said to me one day:

'Is it true, Griet, that there is not one of my children has such a red plush sofa as stands now in Anna's parlour?'

I told her: 'It is true.'

My mother said: 'May God forgive him, Griet, but where does Philip Coetzee get his money?'

And quickly we came to learn where Philip got his money, for that same week he was sued for debt and bonded some of the Brandtwacht lands in payment.

The day that his bond was published in the Cape Town paper Philip bought for Anna a little black box that played three tunes. In the evening, when Ludovic rode by on his horse, Anna was sitting out on the *stoep*. She called to Ludovic, and Ludovic, thinking she meant to speak of the bond, rode up to the *stoep*.

Anna said to him: 'Listen now, Brother, to the music that comes from this little black box that Philip has given me!'

Ludovic said to her: 'Anna, have you seen this day the Cape Town paper?'

Anna answered: 'But no, Brother! Leave now the Cape Town paper and listen to the music that comes from this little black box that Philip has given me.'

And Ludovic, sitting on his horse, looked at Anna and could not believe that she did not know about Philip's bond. He opened his mouth to speak, then closed it again, and turned round his horse and rode away.

From that day Anna came but seldom to Welgevonden, and always when she came Philip Coetzee came with her. Anna took it for love of her that he kept now so close by her side, and her love for him was a fever that all the world might see. Little by little, through her love for him, Philip cut Anna off from us all. And week by week when his bonds were published he would bring some strange new thing from Platkops dorp to please her. So it was that Philip played with our sister Anna till the last of the Brandtwacht lands were bonded. And quickly, quickly then the game was ended.

It happened so that in September month our little Jacoba grew ill, and I took the child to Welgevonden and stayed with my mother there to nurse her. And while I was there Philip brought one day to Brandtwacht a strange young man who was a Jew. Philip said the Jew was his friend, and that Anna must take him over the house and show him the furniture. Anna was proud as a child to do this. She did not know it, and there was not one of us that knew it, but Philip was now a bankrupt and the Jew had come to make a list of all the things that must be sold to pay his debts. Yes, Anna's house and her lands, her cattle and her ostriches, all, all that was hers must now be sold to pay Philip's debts. And even to the day of the sale, which was to be at old Piet Grobelaar's store, there was not one of us that knew it.

The day of the sale, early in the morning before Anna was up, Philip sent his boys with the cattle and the ostriches to old Piet Grobelaar's. When coffee-time came he said to Anna that he had sent the boys for forage and that he must now ride after them. Philip left Anna alone in the house, and on the way to Piet Grobelaar's he met again the strange young man who was a Jew. As they stood talking together in the road brother Ludovic rode by on his horse, and the Jew, who seemed angry about something with Philip, called to Ludovic to stop. At first, because for many months now not one of my brothers had spoken to Philip, brother Ludovic would not stop. But afterwards, God knows how it was, he turned his horse and rode back to the Jew. And the Jew asked him if he were going to old Piet Grobelaar's for the Brandtwacht sale. . . . Yes, that was the first that we knew of the sale.

Standing there in the road, speaking no word to Philip, Ludovic asked the Jew to stop the sale until he could fetch our brothers from their farms and together they would see what could be done to save the Brandtwacht lands. The Jew promised, and Ludovic, riding so hard as he could up the valley to Thys, and on to Rijk and Andries, sent our brothers one by one to Anna's house asking for Philip and the Jew. And always Anna sent them on to old Piet Grobelaar's, where Philip had gone for forage.

Last of all, from Vergelegen, came brother Lombard whom Ludovic had sent a boy to fetch. Lombard asked Anna:

'Where is the sale?'

Anna said to him: 'But, Brother! What is now wrong with our family? First comes Thys and asks for Philip and rides away. And then comes Rijk and asks for Philip and rides away. And then Andries. And now you! What sale is it then that you all ride so hard to?'

Lombard said to her: 'But Anna! Do you not know what Philip is doing?'

Anna said: 'What is he doing? He is fetching forage from old Piet Grobelaar's store.'

Lombard told her: 'God forgive him, Anna, but Philip is selling this day your house and your lands, your cattle and your ostriches, and all that is yours to pay his debts.'

And Lombard, who, like all my brothers, could not believe that Anna did not know about Philip and his bonds whipped up his horse and rode away.

That day my brothers bought back the farm of Brandtwacht among them. And Ludovic and Otto also, who worked always together for good, bought back Anna's furniture and settled it so that Anna should have it as long as she lived. But because not one of my brothers knew that Philip had left my sister Anna, for he left her that day when he rode off with the Jew, there was not one of them that went to Brandtwacht to see her. And all that day, and all that night, Anna sat alone in the grey stone house my father had built for her.

That night, late in the night, Otto and Ludovic came to my mother and me at Welgevonden. They told us all what they had done, and while my mother lay crying quietly in her bed I said to Ludovic:

'But where, then, is our sister Anna?'

Ludovic said: 'Now surely she is at Brandtwacht with her husband Philip.'

I said to him: 'God forgive you, Ludovic, but for a good man you are also a fool. There is not one of us, neither Anna nor another, that will see young Philip Coetzee again until he comes to borrow money.'

And I put the child in the bed with my mother, and made Otto inspan the cart and drive me through the night to my sister Anna.

When we came to the farm at sun-up there was no sound on all the place. I climbed out of the cart and ran through the house and found Anna alone in the parlour. She sat on the red plush sofa and already her cheeks were flushed with the fever that was so soon to kill her. On her lap she held the little black box that Philip had given her, but though she turned and turned the handle there came no sound from it.

I said to her: 'Anna, my darling, our mother waits for you at Welgevonden and I have come to fetch you.'

Anna, who was so dear to us all, looked at me with wild strange eyes that would never again see any of us clearly.

'Listen now, Griet,' she said, 'to the music that comes from this little black box that Philip has given me.'

THE PASTOR'S DAUGHTER

I was teaching school for Miss Cherry in Platkops dorp when Niccoline Johanna told me her love story. Niccoline lived then in the old Bergh house opposite Miss Cherry's garden, and Christoffeline, her little adopted niece, lived with her. Christoffeline was one of my pupils, and it was because of this, I think, that Niccoline made me her friend. Niccoline was a very silent woman, but, like many silent women, as I came afterwards to learn, she could at times speak very freely of all that was on her mind. As we sat sewing together one afternoon, re-making a little white dress for her niece, she said to me suddenly:

'Tell me now! Whose child do they say Christoffeline is?'

'Why, Niccoline,' I cried, 'she is your uncle Hans's child, and her mother died when she was born!'

And Niccoline, putting down her work and looking out across the garden, answered: 'She is not my uncle Hans's child. My uncle Hans had no child. She is Paul Marais's child. Wait! I will now tell you!'

And here is what she told me.

When my father was the pastor of Platkops dorp and I was still a young girl, Paul Marais came down from the Caroline district to farm with old Jan Cloete on the Ghamka river. My father, who had also come from the Caroline district, knew the parents of Paul Marais, and when he came to the dorp the young

64

man would come to see my father at the parsonage. The first time that he came Jan Cloete brought him. Jan Cloete talked with my parents, and I remember yet how his beard waggled, and Paul Marais talked with me. He told me that day that his grandmother had been an Englishwoman. He was very proud of this and made me talk English for exercise. Every time that he came after that he spoke of his grandmother and made me talk English. He was very earnest about it. He was like that about everything that he did. It mattered terribly to Paul that his grandmother had been English, and he made it matter also to me. Yes, he was like that. He nearly always got what he wanted and made you want him to get it. My father was not like that. The only thing that my father had wanted for himself was a daughter and it was not until he had been many years in Platkops that I was born. And then my mother gave me a man's name after my father himself—Niccoline Johanna for Niklaas Jan.

My mother was a very quick-tempered woman and sometimes my father's goodness and patience would drive her nearly mad. My father was for ever giving his things away and trusting in the Lord. My mother could not so easily trust in the Lord and sometimes she would say very bitter things to my father about his patience and his faith, and about the saints in the Bible. And she would say that she who ought to have married Peter had married Moses. My mother could never like Moses. Jacob also she hated, and I remember yet how she would make me cry when she read me the story of Esau crying for the blessing that Jacob had stolen. And yet though she was always quarrelling with my father about the saints in the Bible I know now that my mother was a good woman. It was her illness that made her so bitter and so unhappy, and so afraid for the future. We did not know that she was ill, but she knew, and the year that Paul Marais came she said many terrible things to my father and me, and not anything that we could do would please her. When Paul Marais asked me to marry him I thought at once how glad I should be to get away from my mother. Yes, I loved Paul with all my heart, and yet my love for him made me cruel towards my mother, and I thought that.

Paul's father had bought for him by now a farm in the Transvaal and we were to be married at once and go up-country. I was glad it was to be in the Transvaal. It would take my mother seven days to get to Paul's farm from Platkops dorp, and God forgive me, but when Paul asked me to marry him I thought at once of that. It was as if it must kill me if I could not be alone with Paul. Yes, love is like that—beautiful and cruel and selfish and bitter, and who can tell where the one begins and the other ends?

When it was all settled between Paul and me I went to my mother to tell her. My mother was busy that day in the little room where she kept her linen. I went to her there and closed the door and said: 'Ma, I am going to marry Paul Marais. His father has bought him a farm in the Transvaal and I am going to marry him.'

My mother let fall her work and looked up at me. She did not speak, but when I raised my voice and said again: 'I am going to marry Paul Marais,' she pushed aside her work and put her head on the table and cried like a child that is tired and can go no farther. It frightened me to hear her, and because I was frightened I was even more cruel.

I said to her: 'Ma, cry if you like, but I am going to marry Paul Marais. His father has got him a farm in the Transvaal and I am going to marry him.'

My mother rose from her chair, and she, who had never yet pleaded with me about anything, held out her hands towards me and said:

'Niccoline, do not leave me!'

And God forgive me, but even as she spoke I drew back against the wall and cried: 'But, Ma! I am going to marry Paul Marais!'

For a moment my mother looked at me and then, quickly, she began to undo her bodice. It had many buttons and she breathed hard, like a horse. I thought to myself, 'Surely my mother is now going mad, but I shall marry Paul Marais and live with him in the Transvaal. . . .' Yes, I thought that. . . . My mother undid her slip and pulled down her chemise. And I knew then what it was that she hid there.

My mother said: 'Look, Niccoline!'

But I could not look, and she said again: 'Niccoline, in six months I shall be dead.'

And I heard, but could not speak.

My mother said at last: 'My child, when I am dead and you are with Paul Marais in the Transvaal how will it go with your pa? Your pa is a saint, but like all the saints he is also a fool. When I am dead and you are with Paul in the Transvaal how will it go with him?'

Well I knew how it would go with him! My father was but a child in the ways of the world and never would he learn to care for himself. Well I knew how it would go with him! And speaking no word to my mother I left her and went to my own room. Long, long I sat there, and though it was the night of the Bible-class I did not go. Only when the Bible-class was over I went out and met Paul in the Hoeg Straat. I said to him: 'Paul, so long as my father lives I cannot marry you.'

Paul looked at me and said: 'My God, Niccoline!'

I said: 'Paul, believe me it is for the best. Before God I have promised my mother. When my father is no longer the pastor of Platkops if you send for me I will come to you. But before God I have promised my mother.'

And Paul answered: 'So! One day you promise me one thing and the next day you promise your mother another thing! May God forgive you and your promises, Niccoline Johanna, but surely my grandfather was right when he chose him an Englishwoman for his wife and I will do so also.'

And he left me there in the Hoeg Straat and took his horses out of the coffee-house stables and drove straight out of Platkops dorp and went to his farm in the Transvaal.

When I went back to the parsonage my mother was waiting for me. She looked at me but did not speak. I said to her: 'Ma, it is all arranged between Paul and me. So long as my father is pastor of Platkops I will stay with him. Afterwards I will go to Paul.'

Yes, I said that. It seemed to me right to say it. I knew that I would never now go to Paul, but my mother had not thought of what would become of me after my father died, only of what would become of him after she died. And one day she would think also of me. So I said to her: 'I will go to Paul.'

And my mother took me into her arms and kissed me and said many kind things about Paul. They were true, the things that she said. Yes, far into the night she talked about Paul and it was as if God had taken me up into a high mountain like Moses and was showing me the things that would never be mine.

From that night my mother was very gentle with me and with my father also, and it seemed to me that I had never known her until now. It came that she grew quickly very ill and soon all the district knew that she was dying of cancer. Many people came to us and showed us such kindness as my father had not known in all the forty years that he had been their pastor. Yes. . . . My mother suffered much pain, but the five months that it took her to die were among the happiest in her life and in my father's also.

When my mother had been very ill for about four months my father went one day to Geelboss to preach. He drove alone in his buggy. On the way home, between Geelboss and the Louwrens river, he came upon Jan Steen, with his wife and six children. Jan Steen was drunk like he always was. He was the schoolmaster at Geelboss, but drink had lost him his school and he was trekking now to the dorp with his wife and children. It was a

long way that they had still to go. My father
had helped Jan Steen many times before and he
helped him now again. He put his wife and children
in the buggy and sent them on to the dorp, and
started to walk himself with Jan Steen. Jan was
still very drunk and when they got to the Louwrens
river he pushed my father into the stream and then
he himself fell in and my father had to pull him
out. My father was no longer a young strong man,
and from his struggle with Jan and his wetting in
the stream he was already in a fever when he reached
us at the parsonage. In three days my father was
dead.

All Platkops came to my father's funeral, for in all
the Platkops district there was no man who did not
love him, and Jan Steen borrowed money and bought
his wife a new black dress to wear for it. That day
Jan Cloete told me that Paul Marais had married an
Englishwoman in the Transvaal.

My mother did not live many days after my father.
She did not know that Paul was married, and one
night she said to me:

'Is it not strange, Niccoline, that I who could never
trust in the Lord should die now so happy? Your pa
is already safe in Heaven and soon you will be with
Paul in the Transvaal.'

The next morning, one hour before sun-up, my
mother died. Miss Cherry was sitting up with me.
My mother asked for water and I ran to her with a
little glass. Miss Cherry lifted her up and I held the
glass to her lips. The water ran out of her mouth and
down her chin and on to her breast, and I saw that
my mother was dead.

After my mother died the church council gave to

me the old Bergh house where still I live. I planted
me my garden there and sold the vegetables at the
morning market, and I kept also a cow. I lived so
ten years and had much to thank the Lord for. When
I had been seven years in the Bergh house Jan Cloete
asked me one day at the morning market if I knew
that the wife of Paul Marais had run off with the
Mooidorp postmaster? I asked Jan Cloete if Paul
had any children. Jan Cloete told me 'No'. I went
back to my house and thought many nights and days
about Paul and his English wife. Jan Cloete never
spoke to me of Paul again and there was no one else
that I might ask.

It was now three years after that that there came
one night a knock at the door. Delia was already in
bed and I took the lamp and went myself. It was
Paul Marais who stood there, white in the night like
a dead man.

He said to me: 'Niccoline Johanna, I have come
to ask you to forgive me. My wife is dead and I have
come to ask you to marry me. Will you do this,
Niccoline Johanna?'

I said to him: 'So surely as I live I will do
it!'

And Paul said to me: 'I was at a sale at my
uncle's farm in the Caroline district when my
wife's brother came to me and told me that
my wife was dead and that surely there were
things of hers that belonged now to him. I told
him I would send him the things, but first I must
go to Platkops, and afterwards when it was settled
about the sale I would send him the things.' And
he said to me also:

'It will take me one month to get all settled up,

Niccoline Johanna, and in one month I will come for you and we will go together to the Transvaal.' And I made him a cup of coffee, and he climbed on his horse and rode away.

I cannot tell you what it was like for me after Paul rode away. I could speak to no one about him and yet it seemed to me that all the world must know that in one month he would come to make me his wife. When I went to the Bible-class I tried even to sing, I was so happy. When Magdalena Fourie looked at me with her great flat face I did not feel a fool. I stopped singing, but I thought to myself, 'It is Magdalena who is the fool.'

When it was now three weeks that Paul had been gone I sat one night sewing at the dress that I would wear for my wedding. It was late, and in all the dorp my house alone had a light. Presently there came into the garden a drunk man. The drunk man came on to the *stoep*, and I do not know how it was but I knew then that it was Paul. I ran to the door and called to him. When I got him into the room I saw that it was not drink that was wrong with him but trouble and hunger. I had seen men come to my father like that and I knew. I ran and made coffee, and gave him biltong and bread to eat. I would not let him speak till he had eaten. And then he said to me:

'Niccoline, my wife is alive.' And this is what he told me. . . . Coming down from his farm he had to spend a night at the Watersand toll-house in the Philip district. It was late when he reached the toll and the toll-master was away from home. A coloured boy took his horse to the stable and Paul went straight to his room. The next morning a white woman brought him his coffee. She opened the shutters, and when she turned he saw that it was his wife.

His wife came up to the side of the bed and said: 'Paul Marais, I heard you come last night. You came in answer to prayer. For three years my life has been hell. I ask you now to save me. I don't ask you to forgive me, Paul Marais, but I ask you to save me. If you don't take me away from here I shall kill John Gordon when he comes home, and then I shall kill myself.' And she left him. And Paul saw then how her brother had lied to him so that he might get hold of her things, and he remembered also that the coloured boy who took his horse to the stable had said that his master would be away still three more days.

When Paul remembered this he dressed very quietly and climbed out of the window and went to the stable and got out his horse. In five minutes he was on the road to Platkops dorp and that whole day he had no food. He was weak like a child when he came to me. It was terrible to me to see him so weak. He who had been always so sure of himself did not know now what he must do. He said to me:

'What shall I do, Niccoline Johanna?'

I said to him: 'Paul, can you ask me that? Go back to your wife before it is too late, or surely God will hold you to blame.'

And Paul said, as he had said so many years before: 'My God, Niccoline!'

For a long time I talked with Paul and at last he went away. When I could no longer hear his horse on the road I went to my own room and cried as if my heart must break. And always I said to myself: 'Who was now the fool in the Bible-class, Niccoline Johanna? Was it Magdalena Fourie?' Yes. . . . All that night I saw Magdalena's flat face looking at me when I tried to sing in the Bible-class.

For many days after that I thought I could not live. I could not forget how ill Paul looked, and I trembled all the time to hear that his wife had killed John Gordon. When Delia dropped her pails I thought: 'They have come to tell me.' For the least sound my heart would stop and I would think: 'They have come to tell me.' At the morning market they said to me:

'But you are ill, Niccoline Johanna! What is then wrong with you?' And I could not tell them.

At last one day there came a letter from Paul saying that he and his wife were now in the Transvaal. He was selling his farm and going to another close to where my father's youngest brother, Hans, was then living. His wife also wrote. Yes. . . . Paul had told her all that had happened between us and she wrote to me. It was a sad letter that I got from her, and yet it made me happier than I had been for many weeks.

A good while after that I heard from my uncle Hans that Paul Marais was in consumption and that his wife was expecting a child. I sent Paul a liniment for his chest, and his wife many little things that I made for her baby. His wife wrote that the child was to be called Niklaas Jan if it were a boy, and Niccoline Johanna if it were a girl. I asked them to call it, rather, Christoffeline after my mother.

It was several months after that that my uncle Hans

wrote that Paul Marais had a daughter and that his wife was dead. He said also that Paul could not live the winter through, being now very far gone in consumption. They had got a nurse for the child, but soon, he thought, they would need a nurse also for Paul.

When I read uncle Hans's letter I called to Delia and told her I was going to my uncle in the Transvaal. I went also to Miss Cherry and told her, and we settled it so that she should look after my cow and my garden. Before the rest of the dorp knew about it I was already on my way to the Transvaal in the Platkops post-cart. Miss Cherry said always, to the people who came for milk from my cow, that I had gone to my uncle in the Transvaal.

It was a terrible journey that I took, and when at last I got to my uncle Hans's place Paul was already there with the child Christoffeline. Uncle Hans was kind to all men, as my father had been, and we nursed Paul together. Some days he was very ill, but other days he was sure he was getting better and would give us no peace until we carried him out on the *stoep*. When we got him to the *stoep* he would cry from weakness and ask us to carry him back again to die. Six weeks we nursed him so. The last week of his life he lay with his face to the wall and would speak to no one. But the day that he died he sat up early in the morning, while it was yet dark, and spoke of his grandmother the Englishwoman. All that day he spoke of her and at sundown he died.

After Paul died I came again to Platkops dorp and the child Christoffeline came with me. In Platkops dorp there was not anyone who now remembered Paul Marais. At the morning market they said to me:

'Is it true, Niccoline Johanna, that you have brought a child from your uncle Hans's place to be your adopted niece?'

I told them: 'It is true.'

They said to me: 'May the Lord bless the child to you, Niccoline Johanna!'

And I answered: 'Surely He will do so. . . .'

For a little while after Niccoline Johanna ceased to speak we sat together in silence, and when at last I looked at her, on her strong sallow face there was neither bitterness nor sorrow, only a quiet resignation.

'You see this dress that I am making for Christoffeline?' she said. 'It is the same that I was making that night for my wedding.'

LUDOVITJE

Out on the *stoep* in the moonlight Alida spoke of her son Ludovitje.

See now, she said, how they shine in the night, like stars on the land, the little white flowers in Ludovic's garden. Under the orange-trees he planted them, and always he said: 'For grandfather's grave I will grow them. . . .' And now they grow there for his.

See how it was with my darling! Weak he was from the day he was born, and weak he was all the days of his life, but who was there in all the Platkops district that walked so close with God? When they said to me in Platkops dorp: 'Surely Alida the child is now also weak in his mind?' it was as if my heart must break to hear them. And in the market-place I cried: 'May God forgive us that we have not all such weakness! Full of the grace and glory of God is his mind, and all that know the child may see it.' And I said to them also: 'True it is that Ludovitje goes but seldom to school because of the fever that comes so often upon him, but long ago he has learnt to read, and his book it is the Bible. Yes! The Bible is his reading-book, and tell me now, for stronger minds where is there a greater?'

Yes, so it was that I spoke with them in the market-place. And afterwards, when Maqwasi the Kaffir came many times I thought of it.

The year that grandfather died and Ludovitje planted his garden, that same year it was that my husband, Piet, got a gang of Kaffirs from the Tali district to build him a dam in the Credo mountains.

77

Far up in the mountains they built it, leading the water from there in furrows to our lands in the valley. Piet had often to go to the dam, to see the Kaffirs at their work, and always when he could Ludovitje would go with him. Early, early in the morning they would go, riding together in the stump-cart up our long ravine that lies so beautiful at the foot of the Credo mountains. There was no road for them to go but a track only that the Kaffirs had made, and so rough it was that as they drove the cart would toss and swing like a branch in a storm, and the little kopjes would dance before their eyes. And always then Ludovitje would sing to his father the 114th psalm: 'The mountains skipped like rams and the little hills like young sheep.' Yes, when they sing that psalm in Platkops church* I see again my darling riding to the mountains with his father.

The Kaffirs that worked for Piet were such big strong men as do not belong to our part of the colony. They came from far up-country and they did not yet believe in the Living God, the Heavenly Father. But when Ludovitje came among them, singing his psalm, they would stop in their work to listen to him. And quickly they came also to sing it. Yes, these men that did not yet believe in the Living God, the Heavenly Father, came so, as they builded our dam, to sing the 114th psalm: 'Tremble, thou earth, at the presence of the Lord, at the presence of the God of Jacob, Who turned the hard rock into a standing water and the flintstone into a springing well.'

So they would sing, and Maqwasi, that was the head of the gang, would say to the child, Ludovitje:

* Metrical version used in Dutch church.

'Tell us now! Who is this King of Jacob? And where is now this springing well?'

And Ludovitje would tell him. Of the wanderings of the Children of Israel he would tell him, and of God's guidance in the Wilderness. Of God's goodness and mercy to those that love Him he would tell him, and of the pure River of Water of Life that He has given us.

Maqwasi would say to him: 'Where runs now this River of Water of Life?'

And Ludovitje would answer: 'Clear as crystal is the River of Water of Life and close by the throne of God and of the Lamb it runs.'

Yes, so it was that my darling spoke with Maqwasi the Kaffir, and always he would say to me: 'Wait now! Maqwasi will yet be a pearl in my crown.'

There came a day, when the Kaffirs had nearly finished their work, that Ludovitje grew ill again of his fever and Piet went to the dam alone. When he saw that the child was not with his father Maqwasi came to Piet and said: 'Master! How goes it with the child?'

And Piet said to him: 'The child lies now so sick on his bed that there is not one of us that knows how it will go with him.'

Maqwasi said to him: 'Master! Let Master now give Maqwasi leave to go to the child.'

And Piet answered him: 'Go then!'

So it was that Maqwasi put down his tools and ran from the mountains down the ravine to our farm in the valley. All the way from the mountains he ran, and presently he stood in the door of the room where Ludovitje was lying. Gently he came, but Ludovitje heard him, and sitting up in his bed he held out his

arms and cried: 'Maqwasi! Maqwasi! Clear as
crystal is the River of Water of Life and close by the
throne of God and of the Lamb it runs. Can you not
yet believe, Maqwasi?'

And Maqwasi, standing there with tears in his
eyes, answered him: 'Master! Now I believe.'

Yes, God knows how it was, but from that moment
Maqwasi believed.

All that day, and the next day also, Maqwasi
stayed with us at the farm. When the young doctor
came the next morning from Platkops dorp he
thought at first that Ludovitje was better. But
Ludovitje himself said to Maqwasi: 'This night I
shall see my King.'

All that day the people came from the farms around
us to see the child, for all through the valley it was
known already that Ludovitje had saved Maqwasi
the Kaffir and that he now lay dying. When the
house was now so full of people that many were out
also on the *stoep* there came the teacher from the farm
school and all the scholars with her.

The teacher asked him: 'Shall I sing to you,
Ludovitje?'

And Ludovitje answered: 'Sing now the 114th
psalm, and Maqwasi, that is the pearl of my crown,
will sing it also.'

And she began to sing, and the scholars and
Maqwasi with her, and all the people that were in
the house and on the *stoep*.

And when they had sung 'Tremble, thou earth,
at the presence of the Lord, at the presence of the
God of Jacob Who turned the hard rock into a
standing water, and the flintstone into a springing
well', Ludovitje, who lay with his head on my breast,

cried out aloud: 'A dove! A dove! See now, a dove in the window!'

And we looked, but could see no dove.

And Ludovitje cried again: 'To the River of Water of Life he flies before me! I come, Lord Jesus! I come! I come!'

And he half rose from the bed and held out his arms. And falling again, with his head on my breast, he died.

That night when the child lay in his coffin Maqwasi came to Piet and said: 'Master! Let me now dig a grave for the child on the kopje that lies behind the house and looks towards the mountains. Surely it is towards the mountains that the child would lie.'

Piet said to him: 'The kopje is clay-stone, and who now can dig a grave through clay-stone?'

Maqwasi answered: 'Have I not dug for Master a dam in the mountains, and can I not now, with my tools, dig a grave for the child in the clay-stone?'

So he dug the grave. Like a little room in the clay-stone he dug it, and there we laid the child.

When Maqwasi's work at the dam was done and it was now time for him to go back to the Tali district, Piet went to him and asked him to stay. 'Work now for me on the farm, Maqwasi,' he said, 'and surely for the sake of the child I will deal well with you.'

But Maqwasi answered him: 'Master! For the sake of the child to my own people I must go. To tell them of the River of Water of Life I must go, that they also may be pearls in his crown.'

Yes, back to his own people Maqwasi went, to speak with them of the River of Water of Life. And before he went Piet said to him: 'See now, Maqwasi! All men must die, and what is death that we should fear it? Dig for us now before you go, graves for my wife and me that at the last we may lie one on each side of the child. For it may be that when we came to die there will be no man on all the farm that can dig through the clay-stone like Maqwasi the Kaffir, and where then shall we lie?'

So Maqwasi dug for us graves in the clay-stone. One on each side of the child he dug them, and left us, and went again to his own people, spreading the Word of God among them.

THE SISTERS

MARTA was the eldest of my father's children, and she was sixteen years old when our mother died and our father lost the last of his water-cases to old Jan Redlinghuis of Bitterwater. It was the water-cases that killed my mother. Many, many times she had cried to my father to give in to old Jan Redlinghuis whose water-rights had been fixed by law long before my father built his water furrow from the Ghamka river. But my father could not rest. If he could but get a fair share of the river water for his furrow, he would say, his farm of Zeekoegatt would be as rich as the farm of Bitterwater and we should then have a town house in Platkops dorp and my mother should wear a black cashmere dress all the days of her life. My father could not see that my mother did not care about the black cashmere dress or the town house in Platkops dorp. My mother was a very gentle woman with a disease of the heart, and all she cared about was to have peace in the house and her children happy around her. And for so long as my father was at law about his water-rights there could be no peace on all the farm of Zeekoegatt. With each new water-case came more bitterness and sorrow to us all. Even between my parents at last came bitterness and sorrow. And in bitterness and sorrow my mother died.

In his last water-case my father lost more money than ever before, and to save the farm he bonded some of the lands to old Jan Redlinghuis himself. My father was surely mad when he did this, but he did it. And from that day Jan Redlinghuis pressed him, pressed him, pressed him, till my father did not know which way to turn. And then, when my father's back was up against the wall and he thought he must sell the last of his lands to pay his bond, Jan Redlinghuis came to him and said:

'I will take your daughter, Marta Magdalena, instead.'

Three days Jan Redlinghuis gave my father, and in three days, if Marta did not promise to marry him, the lands of Zeekoegatt must be sold. Marta told me this late that same night. She said to me:

'Sukey, my father has asked me to marry old Jan Redlinghuis. I am going to do it.'

And she said again: 'Sukey, my darling, listen now! If I marry old Jan Redlinghuis he will let the water into my father's furrow, and the lands of Zeekoegatt will be saved. I am going to do it, and God will help me.'

I cried to her: 'Marta! Old Jan Redlinghuis is a sinful man, going at times a little mad in his head. God must help you before you marry him. Afterwards it will be too late.'

And Marta said: 'Sukey, if I do right, right will come of it, and it is right for me to save the lands for my father. Think now, Sukey, my darling! There is not one of us that is without sin in the world and old Jan Redlinghuis is not always mad. Who am I to judge Jan Redlinghuis? And can I then let my father be driven like a poor white to Platkops dorp?' And she drew me down on to the pillow beside her, and took me into her arms, and I cried there until far into the night.

84

The next day I went alone across the river to old Jan Redlinghuis's farm. No one knew that I went, or what it was in my heart to do. When I came to the house Jan Redlinghuis was out on the *stoep* smoking his pipe.

I said to him: 'Jan Redlinghuis, I have come to offer myself.'

Jan Redlinghuis took his pipe out of his mouth and looked at me. I said again: 'I have come to ask you to marry me instead of my sister Marta.'

Old Jan Redlinghuis said to me: 'And why have you come to do this thing, Sukey de Jager?'

I told him: 'Because it is said that you are a sinful man, Jan Redlinghuis, going at times a little mad in your head, and my sister Marta is too good for you.'

For a little while old Jan Redlinghuis looked at me, sitting there with his pipe in his hand, thinking the Lord knows what. And presently he said:

'All the same, Sukey de Jager, it is your sister Marta that I will marry and no one else. If not, I will take the lands of Zeekoegatt as is my right, and I will make your father bankrupt. Do now as you like about it.'

And he put his pipe in his mouth, and not one other word would he say.

I went back to my father's house with my heart heavy like lead. And all that night I cried to God: 'Do now what you will with me, but save our Marta.' Yes, I tried to make a bargain with the Lord so that Marta might be saved. And I said also: 'If He does not save our Marta I will know that there is no God.'

In three weeks Marta married old Jan Redlinghuis and went to live with him across the river. On Marta's wedding day I put my father's Bible before him and said:

'Pa, pray if you like, but I shall not pray with you. There is no God or surely He would have saved our Marta. But if there is a God as surely will He burn our souls in Hell for selling Marta to old Jan Redlinghuis.'

From that time I could do what I would with my father, and my heart was bitter to all the world but my sister Marta. When my father said to me:

'Is it not wonderful, Sukey, what we have done with the water that old Jan Redlinghuis lets pass to my furrow?'

I answered him: 'What is now wonderful? It is blood that we lead on our lands to water them. Did not my mother die for it? And was it not for this that we sold my sister Marta to old Jan Redlinghuis?'

Yes, I said that. It was as if my heart must break to see my father water his lands while old Jan Redlinghuis held my sister Marta up to shame before all Platkops.

I went across the river to my sister Marta as often as I could, but not once after he married her did old Jan Redlinghuis let Marta come back to my father's house.

'Look now, Sukey de Jager,' he would say to me, 'your father has sold me his daughter for his lands. Let him now look to his lands and leave me his daughter.' And that was all he would say about it.

Marta had said that old Jan Redlinghuis was not always mad, but from the day that he married her his madness was to cry to all the world to look at the wife that Burgert de Jager had sold to him.

'Look,' he would say, 'how she sits in her new tent-cart—the wife that Burgert de Jager sold to me.'

And he would point to the Zeekoegatt lands and say: 'See now, how green they are, the lands that

Burgert de Jager sold me his daughter to save.'

Yes, even before strangers would he say these things, stopping his cart in the road to say them, with Marta sitting by his side.

My father said to me: 'Is it not wonderful, Sukey, to see how Marta rides through the country in her new tent-cart?'

I said to him: 'What is now wonderful? It is to her grave that she rides in the new tent-cart, and presently you will see it.'

And I said to him also: 'It took you many years to kill my mother, but believe me it will not take as many months for old Jan Redlinghuis to kill my sister Marta.' Yes, God forgive me, but I said that to my father. All my pity was for my sister Marta, and I had none to give my father.

And all this time Marta spoke no word against old Jan Redlinghuis. She had no illness that one might name, but every day she grew a little weaker, and every day Jan Redlinghuis inspanned the new tent-cart and drove her round the country. This madness came at last so strong upon him that he must drive from sun-up to sun-down crying to all whom he met:

'Look now at the wife that Burgert de Jager sold to me!'

So it went, day after day, day after day, till at last there came a day when Marta was too weak to climb into the cart and they carried her from where she fell into the house. Jan Redlinghuis sent for me across the river.

When I came to the house old Jan Redlinghuis was standing on the *stoep* with his gun. He said to me: 'See here, Sukey de Jager! Which of us now had the greatest sin—your father who sold me his daughter Marta, or I who bought her? Marta who

87

let herself be sold, or you who offered yourself to save her?'

And he took up his gun and left the *stoep* and would not wait for an answer.

Marta lay where they had put her on old Jan Redlinghuis's great wooden bed, and only twice did she speak. Once she said:

'He was not always mad, Sukey, my darling, and who am I that I should judge him?'

And again she said: 'See how it is, my darling! In a little while I shall be with our mother. So it is that God has helped me.'

At sun-down Marta died, and when they ran to tell Jan Redlinghuis they could not find him. All that night they looked for him, and the next day also. We buried Marta in my mother's grave at Zeekoegatt. . . . And still they could not find Jan Redlinghuis. Six days they looked for him, and at last they found his body in the mountains. God knows what madness had driven old Jan Redlinghuis to the mountains when his wife lay dying, but there it was they found him, and at Bitterwater he was buried.

That night my father came to me and said: 'It is true what you said to me, Sukey. It is blood that I have led on my lands to water them, and this night will I close the furrow that I built from the Ghamka river. God forgive me, I will do it.'

It was in my heart to say to him: 'The blood is already so deep in the lands that nothing we can do will now wash it out.' But I did not say this. I do not know how it was, but there came before me the still, sad face of my sister, Marta, and it was as if she herself answered for me.

'Do now as it seems right to you,' I said to my father. 'Who am I that I should judge you?'

DESOLATION

ALIE VAN STADEN was close on seventy-two years old when she went with her son, Stephan, and her motherless little grandson, Stephan's Koos, to Mijnheer Bezedenhout's farm of Koelkuil in the Verlatenheid. She was a short squarely-built woman, slow in thought and slow in movement, with dark brown eyes set deep in a long, somewhat heavy and expressionless face. In her youth her eyes had been beautiful, but there was none who now remembered her youth and in old age she looked out upon the world with a patient endurance which had in it something of the strength and something of the melancholy of the labouring ox.

All her life, save for six months in her girlhood, Alie had lived in the Verlatenheid—that dreary stretch of the Great Karoo which lies immediately to the north of the Zwartkops Mountains and takes its name from the desolation which nature displays here in the grey volcanic harshness of its kopjes and the scanty vegetation of its veld. This grey and desolate region was her world. Here, as the child of poor whites and as the mother of poor whites she had drifted for seventy years from farm to farm in the shiftless, thriftless labour of her class. Here in a bitter poverty she had married her man, borne her children, and accepted dumbly whatever ills her God had inflicted upon her. With her God she had no communion save in the patient uncomplaining fulfilment of His will as the daily circumstances of her life revealed it to her. Prayer was never wrung from her.

That cry of 'Our Father! Our Father!' which comes so naturally to the heart and from the lips of her race never came from hers. Sorrow had been her portion, but this was life as she conceived it, and tearless she had borne it. And now of all her sons Stephan alone was left to her, and already Stephan was suffering from that disease of the chest which had killed first his father and then his three brothers, Koos, Hendrick and Piet.

In her son, the bijwoner Stephan van Staden, there was none of old Alie's quiet endurance of life. The bijwoner could not without protest accept the ills which his God so persistently visited upon him. He was a weak and obstinate man who saw in his God a power actively engaged in direct opposition to himself, and at each fresh blow dealt him by his God he lifted up his voice and cried aloud his injury. At Koelkuil his voice was often thus raised, for here his illness rapidly increased, and here he found in his new master a harsh man made harsher by a drought which had brought him close to ruin.

The drought was in fact the worst that any middle-aged man of the Verlatenheid remembered. When Stephan went as bijwoner to Koelkuil the farm had had no rain for over two years and through all his eighteen months of service with Mijnheer only three light showers fell. Day after day men rose to a cloudless sky and hot shimmering air, or to a dry and burning wind that scorched and withered as it blew. Slowly, steadily, the grey earth became greyer, the bare kopjes barer, the veld itself empty of familiar life. The herds of spring-buck seeking water at the dried-up fountains grew smaller and smaller. The field mice, the tortoises, the meer-kats—all the humbler creatures of the veld—died out of ken. The starving jackal played havoc among the starving sheep. The new-born lamb was killed to save the starving ewe. The cattle, the sheep, the ostriches and the donkeys were drawn in their extremity closer to the abodes of men in their vain search for food. Their lowing and bleating drifted mournfully across the stricken land as slowly, steadily, their famished bodies were gathered into the receiving earth and turned again to the dust from which they had sprung.

In the strain of these months there was constant friction between Stephan van Staden and his master. Nothing done by the one was right in the eyes of the other. Stephan, ill and irritable, was loud in his criticism of Mijnheer. Mijnheer, a ruined man, was unjust in the demands he made of his bijwoner. They came at last to an active open warfare into which all on the farm save old Alie were drawn. From their conflict she alone remained quietly aloof. Sitting on the high stone step in front of the bijwoner's house, gazing in melancholy across the Verlatenheid, she would listen in silence to the arguments of both master and man alike. Stephan's vehemence made him indifferent to her silence. Mijnheer resented and feared it. He read in it a judgment of himself, and who was this Alie, the poor white, that she should judge him? Why did she never speak that he might answer? Of what did she think as she sat there, immovable as God, on the high stone step in front of the door? He did not know, and would never know, but he came in the end to hate this old woman, so strong, it seemed to him, in her silence, so powerful in her patience. And when, in a spell of bitter cold, the bijwoner suddenly died, he thought with relief that now old Alie must go.

It was in the early winter of the fourth year of the drought that Stephan van Staden died, and on the day that he was buried Mijnheer, standing by the graveside, told Alie van Staden that his bijwoner's house would be needed at once for the man who was coming in her son's place. He was, he said, but naturally sorry for herself and the child, but doubtless they had relatives to whom they might go, and she must see for herself that it was impossible for him, a man well-nigh ruined by the drought, to do anything whatever to help her. She must know, also, that her son's illness had made him a poor bijwoner and added much to his losses among his sheep. In fact the more he thought of it the more convinced he was that no other farmer in the Verlatenheid would have borne with Stephan so long as he, Godlieb Bezedenhout, had done. And on this note of righteousness he ended.

To all that Mijnheer had to say Alie listened, as always, in silence. What, indeed, was there for her to answer? Mijnheer spoke of relatives to whom she might turn for help for herself and Stephan's child, but in fact she had none. She was the last of her generation as Stephan had been the last of his. The poor white is poor also in physique, and of all her consumptive stock only Stephan's Koos remained. Stephan's wife had died when her son was born, and her people had long since drifted out of sight, she could not say where. The child, therefore, had none but herself to stand between him and destitution. All that was to be done for him she herself must do. All that was to be planned for him she herself must plan.

Slowly, while her master spoke, these thoughts passed through her mind. But by no word did she betray them or the desolation of her heart. When he ceased she parted from him with a quiet 'Good-day' and went back to the bijwoner's house with Stephan's Koos.

For her six-year-old grandson Alie had a deep but inarticulate tenderness. All the little warmth that life still held for her came to her through Stephan's Koos. It was she who had saved him when Anna died. It was she who had stood between him and the fury of his father when Stephan, in his illness, turned against his own son. All that Stephan's son had known of love had come to him through her, yet for that love she had found no words and to it she could give no expression beyond a rare and awkward gesture, too harsh or too restrained to be called a caress. Yet the boy—a slim small child with eyes as dark as her own, and long thin fingers like the claws of a bird—was conscious of no shortcomings in his grandmother. His father had always been strange to him, and death had but added another mystery to the many which had surrounded him in life. But with his grandmother nothing was strange or mysterious. With his grandmother he knew where he was going, he knew what he was doing. She was his tower of strength, his shadow of a great rock in a dry and thirsty land. By her side he was safe. Wherever she went, whatever she did, by her side he was safe. . . .

When they reached the house Alie sat down, as was her custom, upon the high stone step in front of the door, and the boy, pressing close to her side to deepen his sense of security there, sat down beside her. For a time they were silent, the child content, his grandmother brooding on the past. She was a woman of little imagination. Her mind, moving slowly among familiar things, was heavy always with the melancholy of the Verlatenheid, and from it she had but one escape—to the village of Hermansdorp where once as a girl she had lived with her mother's cousin, Tan' Betje, and worked with her at mattress-making at one of the stores. Beyond this her thoughts never ventured. And it was to Hermansdorp that her thoughts travelled slowly now with their dawning hope.

Before them, as they sat on the step, there stretched for mile after mile the grey and barren veld, the wild and broken kopjes of the Verlatenheid. But it was not these that old Alie saw. Her vision travelled slowly, painfully through the years to the long low line of hills to the north, in a fold of which lay the village, with near it, in the shade of a clump of thorn-trees, a dam where men and women journeying to the dorp for Sacrament, outspanned their carts and wagons. She saw again the whitewashed church, and the graveyard, with its tall dark cypress-trees among the whitewashed tombs, where she and Tan' Betje had walked together on Sunday afternoons spelling out the names of those who lay buried there. She saw again the long wide straight Kerk Straat, with its running furrows of clear water and its double row of pear-trees in blossom. Behind the pear-trees were whitewashed dwelling-houses set back in gardens or green lands, and stores with *stoeps* built out on to the street under the trees. At the head of the street, across it, stood the square whitewashed gaol—and she remembered how, when first she had seen it, not knowing it to be the gaol, there had come into her mind that saying of our Lord: 'In my Father's house are many mansions'—so big and gracious had this building seemed to her.

Tan' Betje's little house, she remembered, had been up a narrow lane. Three rooms it had had, with green wooden shutters, and a pear-tree in the yard. Under the pear-tree they had sat together cleaning the coir for mattresses—dipping it first into buckets of hot water, then teasing it and spreading it out in the sun to dry. For the poor they had made mattresses of mealie-leaves, stripping the dried leaves into shreds with a fork and packing them into sacks. . . . It had been pleasant in the yard, and Tan' Betje's talk pleasant to hear. And in the little house there had always been food. She could not remember a day when there had not been food. Good food. Tan' Betje had been kind to her, and at the store too they had been kind. Her master's son had himself come several times to speak to her when she went for the coir. The old master would be dead now, perhaps. But the young master would be there. And he would remember. He would give her work. . . .

As if following her thoughts her fingers, stiff with labour and old age, fell awkwardly into the once familiar movements of teasing the coir in the sunlit yard. The boy, wearied at last of her long silence, pressed closer to her side. She looked down upon him sombrely and drew his thin, claw-like hand into hers. Slowly, halting often in her speech, she began to talk to him of Hermansdorp where together they would go. And into the child's sense of security there came a new sense of romance and adventure, deepening his confidence in the wisdom and rightness of all that his grandmother said and did.

That night, while her grandson slept, old Alie bundled together their few possessions. Mijnheer had given her three days in which to make her plans and preparations, but she needed in her poverty less time than that for these. Stephan had come to Koelkuil a poor man and he had died a poorer, and in the meagre plenishing of the bijwoner's house there was little that could not be piled on to the rough unpainted cart by which, eighteen months earlier, they had journeyed to the farm. At dawn she roused the boy and with his help loaded the cart and inspanned the two donkeys. The donkeys were poor and starved, as were also the pitiful handful of sheep and goats which were all that remained of Stephan's flock. These, when all was ready, Koos drove out of the kraal towards her. And slowly, as the sun rose, they set off.

As they left the farm—the boy on foot herding the little flock, his grandmother perched high on the cart peering out upon the world from the depths of her black calico sunbonnet—there was little to mark their exodus as differing from any other that one might meet at any time in the Verlatenheid. The poor white here, though he belongs to the soil, has no roots in the soil. He is by nature a wanderer, with none of that conservative love of place which makes to many men one spot on earth beloved above all others. Yet the range of his wanderings is limited, and the Verlatenheid man remains as a rule in the Verlatenheid, dwelling in no part of it long, and coming, it may be, again and again for short spells at a time to the farms which lie, for no clear reason, within the narrow course he sets himself.

For old Alie there was no longer any such course

by which she might steer the rough unpainted cart across the wide stretches of the Verlatenheid. The graves of her sons were now the only claims she held there, and to the vision of old age these graves were become but dwindling mounds of earth in a grey and desolate veld which treasured no memories. The bitter freedom of the poor and the bereft was hers. But it was without bitterness that she accepted it and, uncomplaining, took the road to Hermansdorp.

Throughout the first day it was in the Verlatenheid, with frequent outspans, that they journeyed. And here, from sun-up to sun-down they met no human being and saw in the distance only one white-washed and deserted farmhouse, bare and treeless in the drought-stricken veld. Every *kuil* or water-hole they passed was dry, and near every *kuil* were the skeletons of donkeys and sheep which had come there but to perish of their thirst. Of living things they saw only, now and then, a couple of *koorhan* rising suddenly in flight, or a lizard basking lazily in the sun. And once, bright as a jewel in that desert of sand and stone, they came upon a small green bush poisonous to sheep and cattle alike.

On the following day they struck the Malgas-Hermansdorp road and, turning north, left the Verlatenheid behind them. The country ahead of them now was flat as a calm grey sea, its veld unbroken by any kopje until the long low line of the Hermansdorp hills was reached. Yet in the shimmering heat of noon this sea became a strange fantastic world that slipped into being, vanished, and slipped into being again as they gazed upon it. Around them now were ridges of hills where no hills could be, banks of trees where no trees grew, and water that was not water lying in sheets and lakes out of which rose strange dark islands and cliffs. For these phenomena old Alie had neither explanation nor name. They were indeed less clear to her than they were to the boy. But to him their very mystery brought an added sense of his own personal security. Whatever amazing and inexplicable things the distance, like the future, might hold, here, on the Hermansdorp road with his grandmother in the cart by his side, he was safe.

Yet already, as his grandmother well knew, their margin of safety on the Hermansdorp road was narrowing. Though on that second day they reached a water-hole in which, surrounded by deep slime, there still remained a small pool at which she could water her flock and her donkeys, by nightfall three of her sheep had died by the roadside and she knew that she must lose more. The veld here, though less bare than that of the Verlatenheid, yielded no grazing for them, and the longer the journey the less could she save. Yet in their weakness she dare not press them, and their progress was broken now by more and more frequent outspans which meant no food as well as no water for her donkeys and sheep, no food as well as no coffee for herself and Koos. The water in the water-cask which hung below the cart must be dealt out sparingly if it were to carry them to the end of their journey, and there had been little to pack into the tin canister of food when they set out. This she explained to Koos when, after lighting a fire of dried-up bushes, she put on no kettle to boil for coffee. The boy accepted her ruling as she herself accepted the ruling of God. All, he felt, would be right when they reached Hermansdorp.

It was on the morning of the third day that they came within sight of the township, lying, as old Alie remembered it, in a fold of the hills. In the cold bright winter air its whitewashed buildings stood out clearly against their dark background, and the boy forgot for a moment his increasing hunger and burst into eager questioning. His grandmother answered him slowly, patiently, her thoughts on the dam outside the village where she would water her donkeys and sheep.

This day, however, was the hardest and most tedious of their journey. Many hours passed before they reached the dam and in these hours more of the sheep died and the going of the donkeys became a painful somnambulistic crawl. To ease their burden of her weight old Alie left her seat in the cart and walked by the side of the patient suffering beasts, calling them quietly by name. From time to time they turned towards her seeking with their tongues such moisture as her clothes might hold. And always when they did so she would speak to them quietly, as if speaking to children, of the Hermansdorp dam.

The dam lay about three miles to the south of the township, and for over fifty years men journeying to the village for market or the Sacrament had watered their flocks and spans here, and made it their last outspan on entering the dorp, their first upon leaving it. It had been, too, the general picnic place of the village, and all old Alie's memories of it were stirring and gay. But as at last they neared it in the fading light of that winter afternoon there crept into her heart a sombre foreboding. The thorn-trees around it were not, as she had remembered them, laden with the scented golden balls of spring, for this was winter, and in winter they must be bare. But she knew before she reached them that they were bare not because winter had made them so but because drought had killed them. And she needed no telling, though a small dark girl broke away from an inspanned wagon, standing solitary beneath the trees, to cry the news aloud, that the dam was dry.

In the bitter wind of winter drought, which all day long had blown across the veld, these barren trees, this empty sunbaked hollow gaping to the indifferent heavens, this eager child triumphant with disaster, brought desolation to old Alie as it had never been brought to her in the familiar world of the Verlatenheid. Yet she gave no sign that her strength of mind and of body were well-nigh spent, but, wheeling the donkeys off the road, began patiently to outspan. As she did so there came towards her from the wagon a tall dark man smoking a pipe, and a cheerful round-faced woman carrying a child in her arms.

These strangers gave her greeting, and the man, beginning at once to help her, fell into easy friendly talk. It was true, he said, that there was no water in the dam, and never before had any man seen it so. If Mevrouw needed water and food for her donkeys and sheep there was none to be had until one reached the coffee-house in Hermansdorp. But it was clear that Mevrouw could take her sheep and donkeys no farther now. Let her rest then at the fire he had made for his wife, and which they were just leaving, and he would see what he could do for her.

Old Alie thanked him and asked his name. He was, he said, Jan Nortje, bijwoner to Mijnheer Ludovic Westhuisen of Leeukuil, and this was

Marta his wife. He had been to the dorp on business
for his master and was now on his way back to the
farm. Had Mevrouw come from far, and had she
far to go? It looked to him as if she had made a hard
journey.

From Koelkuil in the Verlatenheid, answered old
Alie, where but three days ago she had buried her
son, the father of her little Koos here. And to
Hermansdorp they were now going.

Then surely, said Jan Nortje, Mevrouw had
journeyed in sorrow. But let her go now and sit with
his wife by the fire and drink coffee and he would
see to her donkeys and sheep.

With the numbed docility of utter weariness Alie
obeyed him and, holding Koos by the hand, followed
Marta to the fire. Here, handing the baby over to
the child who had first run out to greet them, Jan
Nortje's wife busied herself about her guests, putting coffee and food before them. She was a plump
motherly young woman, many years her husband's
junior, and in her pleasant soothing voice there was
a persuasive kindliness which made old Alie think of
her mother's cousin Tan' Betje. Just in the same
gentle and pitying way had Tan' Betje mourned over
the sorrows of others. Was it but three days ago,
asked Jan Nortje's wife, that Ou-ma had buried her
son? Our Father! And this was his only child?
And an orphan? Then surely the hand of the Lord
had been heavy upon her! But upon whom was His
hand not heavy in this bitter time of drought?
Throughout all the land was ruin and desolation such
as no man living remembered. Turn where one
would there was sorrow. Men that had been rich
were now poor, and those that had been poor were

now starving, taking their children like sheep to be fed at the orphan-house in Hermansdorp. It was to the orphan-house that they had been that day with gifts from Mijnheer and Mevrouw at Leeukuil. The pastor had asked that all who could do so should send food and clothing to the orphan-house for those in need, and several times now Mijnheer had sent Jan Nortje in with the wagon. Was it perhaps to the orphan-house that Ou-ma was taking the child?

To the orphan-house? repeated old Alie vaguely. No, it was not to the orphan-house she was going. It was to Canter's store. To work there at mattress-making.

Was Ou-ma then a mattress-maker? asked Jan Nortje's wife in wonder. And where was this Canter's store?

At the head of the Kerk Straat, answered old Alie. Close by the gaol.

Was Ou-ma sure?

Sure? asked old Alie sombrely. How could she be but sure? Had she not worked there with her mother's cousin Tan' Betje?

In her answers, as in her silence, there was that quiet aloofness which had so baffled Mijnheer Bezedenhout, and Jan Nortje's wife said no more. There was no such store as Canter's in the Kerk Straat, nor had there ever been within her memory. But who was she that she should disturb the faith of old age? In Hermansdorp Ou-ma must surely have friends, or why should she go there? And they would see how it was with her. . . . She turned, smiling, to the boy. His little eager face was pinched with hunger and cold, but his eyes were bright, his spirit still adventurous, his safety still assured. For him, she knew, Canter's store was where his grandmother said it was—at the head of the Kerk Straat, close to the gaol. And who was she that she should disturb the faith of childhood?

She had turned to more practical matters and was packing some food into a canister for Ou-ma and the boy when Jan Nortje rejoined them. He had, he said reloaded Mevrouw's cart so that its weight should be more evenly balanced, and he had done what he could for her sheep, but it was doubtful if more than four of them could reach the dorp. As things were Mevrouw had better spend the night here and set off again at dawn. He wished much that he could have done more for her, but doubtless in Hermansdorp she had friends who would help her. And now, as it was already late, he himself must be moving. . . .

When Jan Nortje and his wife had left them and the sound of their wagon wheels had died away into the swiftly gathering darkness old Alie settled down with the boy before the fire. Warmed and comforted he soon fell asleep, but for her there was no sleep, no escape from her weariness, no relief to her melancholy. Throughout the long night pain crept through her body with the quiet gentle insistence of a slowly rising tide. By no effort of will and no physical means within her power could she stem it. In her discomfort her mind fell into a confusion of thought for the future and memory of the past. It was now Tan' Betje's voice that she heard, speaking of work to do for Canter's store. It was now Jan Nortje's wife who spoke, telling of the orphan-house in Hermansdorp. Out of the darkness beyond the firelight the orphan-house and the store took shape in her thoughts, vanished and took shape again as the mirages in the veld had done in the heat of the previous noon. When dawn came it was in weariness of body and with mind unrested that she roused herself to the labours of a new day and set off for the coffee-house.

The coffee-house in Hermansdorp, one of the oldest houses in the village, was a long, gabled, yellow-washed building at the lower end of the Kerk Straat. Its yard stood open to the street, and here, as in the market-square, carts and wagons were outspanned by those who came to the dorp for the quarterly Sacrament or the weekly market. In good seasons Andries Geldenhuis and his wife did brisk trade with their coffee and cakes, but in this time of drought there were few with money to spend, and those who outspanned at the coffee-house now were those who had been driven in distress from their lands to seek help from their church, or relief from the government. Among these, when she reached the village at noon, old Alie with her grandson, her rough, unpainted cart, her exhausted donkeys and famishing sheep, took her place almost unnoticed. Only with Andries himself did she have speech. And to him, when her sheep and donkeys had been watered and fed, she said briefly that she had business at the head of the Kerk Straat: that tomorrow she would be selling her sheep and her donkeys at the morning market: and that after the sale she would pay him what was due.

In spring, when the pear-trees which lined it were in blossom against the dark background of the enfolding hills, the wide straight Kerk Straat in

Hermansdorp had an enchanting beauty, and it was in spring that, as a young girl, old Alie had first seen it. Today, like the thorn-trees at the dam, the trees were bare, and the furrows at their roots all waterless. In the open roadway the dust lay deep in ruts, and here, as in the veld, the wind which raised the dust in stinging blinding clouds had the bitter cold of winter drought. Against the wind and the flying dust old Alie's progress was slow. There was, it seemed to her now, no part of her body which was not in pain. As she leant on his shoulder for a moment her hand felt hot to Koos through his jacket and shirt. She spoke little, but the boy who had never seen the Kerk Straat in spring and to whom the bare trees, the stir of life, the shops, the houses, the very dust brought an enchantment of their own, was unconscious of her silence. This was not perhaps the Hermansdorp his grandmother had described—but that, as yet, he had hardly realized. Here was romance. Here was adventure. And here still, at his grandmother's side, was safety.

They came presently to a high, long, white-washed wall and here his grandmother halted. Over the top of the wall the boy could see row upon row of straight slender trees, all a dull rusty brown—cypress-trees killed by the drought. Between the trees, out of his sight, were the whitewashed tombs among which in her youth old Alie had wandered. But what had been a garden to her then was now a wilderness in the drought and she turned heavily away.

Beyond the graveyard came the church and the parsonage, and dwelling-houses set back in deep gardens or built close on the street with *stoeps* slightly raised above the side-walk. Fifty years had brought little change to these, but at the upper end of the street where the business of the dorp was carried on, only the old whitewashed gaol was as she remembered it. And here, when at last they reached the grey stone buildings which now surrounded the gaol, she searched for Canter's store in vain. That it still existed she could not bring herself to doubt. And as the signs above the doorways meant nothing to her—for without Tan' Betje's help she could not spell them out—she entered the building which stood, as far as she could judge, where Canter's once had stood and asked to see the master.

A young man was appealed to and came forward pleasantly to ask what he could do for her. She said again that she wished to see the master, and was told that he himself was the master.

Was his name Canter? she asked. And was answered that it was Isaacs.

Was not this then Canter's store?

The young man repeated that it was Isaacs's. There was, he said, no Canter's store in Hermansdorp nor any family of that name, though there might well have been before his time. But what was it that she had wished to buy at Canter's store? No doubt, whatever it was, he himself, Isaacs, would be able to supply it.

Old Alie answered that she had not come to buy but to seek for work. Many years ago she had worked here, at Canter's store, at mattress-making, and it was such work she sought now. Could Mijnheer perhaps employ her?

That, said the young man, was impossible. Mattresses were sent to him ready-made from wholesale stores in Cape Town, and no stores in Hermans-dorp now made their own. But was she sure that there was nothing he could sell her? Prints? . . . Calicoes? A warm shawl, let down in price because of the drought? A coat for the boy?

There was nothing. Aloof, patient, giving no sign of the blow that had fallen upon her, old Alie waited for the young man to cease, then bade him a quiet good-day and left the store.

Out in the wind-swept street she paused, and the boy, conscious for the first time of some hesitation in her movements, looked up at her anxiously. In the store he had heard nothing of the young man's talk with his grandmother, for his mind had been held by the strange and wonderful things displayed around him there. But now suddenly, in his grand-mother's hesitation, came his first hint of insecurity, and with it romance died out of the long bare Kerk Straat in which they stood forlorn. Quickly his hand slipped again into hers. She looked down upon him vaguely, strangely, and saying no word moved heavily down the street.

Against the wind, on their way to the store, their progress had been slow, but it was slower than ever now. What now must she do for the child? Where now must she turn for work? Andries Geldenhuis had said that in the morning market donkeys were sold for a shilling and less, for who in this drought could afford to feed donkeys? And sheep, he had said, in such poor condition as hers, could bring her but little more. When these and the cart were sold she would have money perhaps for a few days' shelter and food at the coffee-house—but after-wards. . .?

She could not see what was to come afterwards. . . .
Yet the boy must have food. At Tan' Betje's little
house there had always been food. Good food. If
she could find Tan' Betje's house now there might
still be people there who remembered her—Betje
Ferreira, the mattress-maker. And they, perhaps,
might help her. . . .

In their slow progress they had come now to the
opening of a lane which ran from the Kerk Straat to
the upper street, and it was up such a lane that Tan'
Betje had lived. Right at the head of the lane the
house had stood . . . and to the head of the lane she
would go.

To the head of the lane they went in silence—and
came not to the whitewashed green-shuttered house
of Betje Ferreira, the mattress-maker, but to a plain
double-storeyed building in a bare wide playground.
Here boys and girls together, some Koos's age, some
older and some younger, were playing at ball. In a
corner of the playground, against a sunny wall, sat a
young girl of twenty, sewing. From time to time the
children appealed to her in their play, or were joined
by her in their laughter. In the cookhouse, close to
the main building, the midday meal was being prepared, and from the house itself came the clatter of
plates being set out on a long trestle table by a
coloured girl who sang at her work.

Slowly, as she halted with Koos in front of the
fence, these sights and sounds impressed themselves
upon old Alie's mind. The talk of Jan Nortje's wife
came back to her. This, then, was the orphan-house.
This, then, was where the children of the poor were
taken to be fed. . . . At first her mind grasped
nothing but this. . . . Then slowly she began to

reason. If she could not find work how could she feed Koos? And where was she to find work in a place where mattresses were no longer made? How was she now to plan for the child? He, too, like these others, must have food. And here, for the asking—had not Jan Nortje's wife said it?—was food.

For herself old Alie had at that moment no thought. What she herself would do if she left the boy here, and where she herself would turn for food were questions which simply did not arise in her mind. Nor, in her ignorance of the ways of the world, did it occur to her that certain formalities might have to precede a child's acceptance at the orphan-house. With no note from the pastor, no order from any of those who supported the orphan-house, but with Koos's hand held close in her own, she pushed open the gate and entered the yard.

From the seat against the wall the young girl came forward quickly to greet her. Had Mevrouw come to leave the child with them? she asked. The pity then was that Juffrouw Volkwijn was not here to receive him. Only she herself, Justine de Jager, was here—in charge for the day. But if it was all in order that the child was to come to them, would Mevrouw leave him and come again herself in the evening to see Juffrouw Volkwijn? Would it suit Mevrouw to do so?

She spoke at a rush, giving no pause for answer. That old Alie had come with the necessary note of admission she never doubted and did not stop to question. Her eager nature had little time for formality of any kind. Let Koos—Koos was his name? Koos van Staden?—let Koos take his place as the children lined up for the midday meal—the bell was just about to ring—and let Mevrouw come again in the evening. . . .

As she spoke the bell rang. Instantly the children ceased their play and formed into line, the girls in one row, the boys in another. Taking him quickly but not unkindly by the shoulder Justine pushed Koos into place at the end of the row of boys. At a sharp word of command from her the girls filed into the house, the boys followed. At the doorway Koos lagged, looking back in bewilderment and appeal to his grandmother. Again Justine seized him by the shoulder and pushed him into the room before her. The door closed, but through the open windows old Alie could hear the tramp of feet on the bare carpetless floor: then silence: then the raising of sweet clear shrill voices in the children's grace—'Thanks to our Father now we give.' . . . She turned and made her way with slow heavy steps to the gate.

It was long past the dinner hour when old Alie at last reached the coffee-house and crossed the yard to her outspanned cart. As she passed them two women seated near a wagon gave her greeting. She made no answer. The women exchanged glances. Who was she then, this old woman who was too proud to return their greeting? For a moment or two they watched her curiously, resenting, as Mijnheer Bezedenhout had resented, her aloofness—then fell again to their talk.

Unaware of their glances as she had been of their greeting old Alie sat down on her low folding-stool. The pain which had racked her limbs throughout the previous night and throughout the morning had given way now to a numbness which made it difficult for her to control her movements, and she sat awkwardly on the stool, seeking such support as she could get from the wheel at her back. Her hands lay idle on her lap, and from the depths of her black calico sunbonnet her dark eyes looked out upon a world that was growing each moment more strange and unreal to her. It was not the coffee-house yard that she saw. It was the Verlatenheid: it was the orphan-house: it was Canter's store: it was Tan' Betje's little house with the pear-tree in the yard. But always, whatever it was, it was Koos's face turned towards her in bewilderment and appeal— adding sorrow to her sorrow. . . . The young girl, Justine, ought not to have parted them so, closing the door between them. But surely she had meant no harm. And presently, when it came towards evening, she, Alie, would go back to the orphan-house and explain to him that she must leave him there until she found work. . . . Just a little while she would leave him, and then, when she had found work, she would come for him again and they would go together to Tan' Betje's little house. Up some other lane it must be, but she would find it. A little house with green shutters and a pear-tree in the yard . . . buckets under the pear-tree . . . and coir spread out in the sun. . . .

Once again the bent fingers began to play in her lap—teasing the coir as once long ago she had teased it: dipping it into the bucket at her side: shaking it: teasing it: spreading it out in the sun to dry. . . .

One of the women seated by the wagon, chancing to look up, saw this strange play, watched it for a moment, then rose and ran towards the cart. She shook old Alie's shoulder gently and spoke to her. 'Ou-ma, are you ill? Are you ill then, Ou-ma?'

Old Alie did not hear. A little while longer she played with the coir—teasing it, plucking it—then at last her fingers grew still.

THE FATHER

Piet Pienaar of Volharding was a harsh, grasping, hard-working, bitter-minded man of sixty, whose wife Aantje had been reduced in the first months of their marriage to complete submission to his will, and whose son Klaas was still, at twenty-seven, an unpaid labourer in his father's lands. His farm, which he had bought *morgen* by *morgen* through years of labour and scrimping and saving, and which he himself had named 'Perseverance', was one of the poorest and one of the smallest in the Magerplatz region of the Platkops district. It lay like a narrow wedge driven towards the river between the farms of richer men, and the homestead—a low, mud-walled building which time seemed never to draw into the surrounding landscape—stood bare and harsh in the bare grey veld.

In build Piet was a big and heavy man, with a full, heavy, black-bearded face and dark brown eyes whose glance betrayed the habitual suspicion and resentment of his thoughts. Though he had learned with difficulty how to reckon those savings in silver and gold with which, every few years, he sought to purchase from his richer neighbours a little more land to add to his own, he could neither read nor write, nor had he ever allowed his son Klaas to learn to read and write. Such learning, he held, not only cost money but lost money, and he looked upon it with fear and suspicion. There was, in fact, no quality or achievement possessed or attained by others than himself which Piet Pienaar did not resent or suspect. In the Magerplatz he risked friendship with no man, and even from his wife and his son did he instinctively withhold his thoughts.

Aantje Pienaar, plump and youthful when Piet married her, was a thin and colourless woman of fifty. Her hair, her skin, her eyes, her clothes all seemed faded alike to toneless shades of the dull grey earth of the Magerplatz in drought. She belonged, as Piet himself had belonged, to those whom others called 'poor whites', and neither in life nor in her surroundings did she ever strike a note of her own. And only in one thing, since the early months of their marriage, had her obedience to her husband's wishes failed. Though Piet had married her so that she might bear him a regiment of sons to win him riches by their unpaid labour in his lands Klaas was her only child.

For the poverty of her womb Piet had never forgiven his wife—and never forgiven his God. Against his God he had harboured—and still har- boured—the resentment of a victim with no direct means of redress. But with Aantje revenge, if not redress, had been quickly possible; and through all their years of toil together Aantje, with the sons she had failed to bear him marshalled in judg- ment against her, had been his unprotesting slave. In his house as in his lands she had laboured from dawn to dark, from week to month, from month to year, with no word of praise or of thanks from the man whom, by his own declaration, she had wronged. Once she may have been aware of the injustice of this serfdom, but she was aware of it no longer. Once she may have prayed for the sons denied her, but she prayed for nothing now. What would one have of life? If the wind blew cold then one was cold. If the wind blew hot then one was hot. One could not heat the wind nor cool it. One could not call forth the wind nor still it. One could but endure it as, by the will of the Lord, it blew across the earth.

So, without bitterness, under Piet's harsh rule, Aantje had come to reason, but reasoning played little part in her son's quiet acceptance of his lot. His patience and endurance, in outward seeming so like her own, were not, like hers, the heavy fruit of a broken spirit but the natural habit of his mind. Klaas had been born his father's slave as he had been born his father's son. Bondage was his by inheritance, and the failure of brothers to follow him into the world to share it had doubled and trebled his bondage. Yet neither in youth nor in manhood had he rebelled against this slavery or questioned his father's right to it.

It was, strangely, this very quality of acquiescence which Piet most resented and feared in his son. Klaas's obedience, it seemed to him, was yielded too easily to his demand. Aantje's had been won only after a battle which, short as it was, had yet been sharp enough to bring him a sense of victory. Klaas's having needed no battle, brought him, rather, a sense of frustration. And, frustrate, Piet came at times almost to hate his willing docile son—to hate his tall spare body, his pale mild grey eyes, his dust-coloured hair: to hate the slow quiet voice which was heard so seldom in speech and was never heard in protest: to hate even his very efficiency. Klaas was a good farmer, a sure and steady worker and wise in his understanding of the Magerplatz soil—but there were times when Piet would have hated him less had he been a bad one. He could then have grappled with him in the battle of argument and come so, because battle was to him the natural means of intercourse with his fellowmen, to understand him. But with Klaas there was neither battle of ideas nor battle of wills, and this one son whom he had begotten remained a stranger to him. As the willow to the wind he bowed to his will and so eluded him.

It was, in fact, through his lands alone that life, at sixty, held any satisfaction for Piet Pienaar—and for his lands he had that narrow and passionate love which in some men is born of a long-starved sense of possession. Coming to the Magerplatz as a young man with nothing but the clothes that he wore he had, by labour and saving, by foresight and scheming, and by the ungrudged toil of his wife and his son, raised himself slowly above the station of the poor white and made this portion of the earth his own. And dreary as the Magerplatz was—its very name meant 'meagre'—all the beauty of the world for Piet lay in his own Volharding.

The farm lay, as did all other farms in the Magerplatz region, in a bare flat plain, unbroken by kopje or hill, through which ran the Grauwklips River. To the north, through the greater Platkops plain into which the Magerplatz merged, there rose, in the distance, dark and serene, the long range of the Zwartkops Mountains. To the south, across the river one came quickly to the broken foothills of the Teniquotas—grey, pink, mauve, blue and red in the varying light, desolate and beautiful, as rich in colour as they were bare of vegetation, wild and volcanic. Among these waterless hills there were no farms, and what had first tempted men to settle in the plain below was now a mystery. But here men had settled and here, though the poverty of the soil had made them name it grimly the 'Magerplatz', they had remained.

In the wide Platkops district this was one of the poorest of all the cultivated regions, and it was perhaps the cheapness of the land here which still drew men to it. Yet no Magerplatz man would ever willingly admit the poverty of the Magerplatz soil. It was not the soil that failed them, they held, but the Grauwklips River, the rains, the seasons, the Lord Himself, who visited them with locusts and rinderpest, horse-sickness and drought. And among Magerplatz men none had greater faith in the soil itself than Piet Pienaar of Volharding, whose farm was poorer in water and water-rights than any other, and whose narrow wedge of land, driven steadily south towards the river in his slow and painful purchase of it, had come as yet only to Mijnheer van Reenen's boundary.

The van Reenen lands—a small portion of a larger farm taken over by Mijnheer Andries van Reenen in payment of a debt, and left by him to the indifferent care of a humble relative of his wife known in the Magerplatz as 'old Oom Phanse'—were the secret goal of all Piet's present strivings. With these lands, which would bring him to the river, Volharding would be not a wedge in shape but a hammer— and with this hammer, and its water-rights, Piet was convinced that riches could be won, and the Lord's injustice to him in the matter of sons be brought to nought, by the growing of Kombuis tobacco. Though Oom Phanse had done nothing with it, and though few men in fact did well with it in the

Magerplatz, Piet himself had long believed that in certain hands Kombuis tobacco could be grown here to profit. But he had spoken his conviction to no man. It had suited his purpose better that no experiments should be tried by old Oom Phanse. Let Mijnheer, a wealthy man who owned various farms in other parts of the district, believe that the soil here was as poor as old Oom Phanse, a fool and an interloper, declared it. The more old Oom Phanse grumbled to Mijnheer, and the greater his failure, the less could Mijnheer demand for his lands when he, Piet, went with his savings to bargain with him for their purchase. And his savings were now close on the sum which had been quoted to him in the Platkops market as the value of the van Reenen lands.

Of the extent of his savings and the range of his ambitions neither Klaas nor Aantje was aware. His miserliness was the habit of a lifetime, and his bitter secretiveness a natural instinct which was growing stronger with increasing years. The sums which he had brought home from the Platkops market, and their hiding-place—for like many other Platkops men he trusted no bank—were known to himself alone. His economies were accepted without question. And when that turmoil of exultation and anxiety, which the thought of the approaching realization of his dreams aroused in him, drove him to yet harsher economies, his excuse, unsought and unspoken, lay clear before them in the devastation of the drought.

The drought was, indeed, one of the most serious of recent years—but in his present mood Piet welcomed it grimly. Not only did it give him excuse for further economies, but it lowered, for the moment, the value of the van Reenen lands and so brought the possibility of their purchase nearer. And it encouraged also old Oom Phanse in his discontent. As the hot dry days of autumn slipped into the cold dry days of winter, and April slipped into May without bringing the rains which would make ploughing possible, Piet nourished and fostered the old man's dissatisfaction whenever, where their lands met, chance brought them together. And he so contrived it that through these anxious weeks chance often brought them together. Saying little himself he would draw the foolish old man into talk and when they parted it would seem to Oom Phanse that in all things he and Piet Pienaar thought alike. Yes, as he went back to his house, an excited and foolish and indignant old man, it would seem to Oom Phanse that Piet Pienaar thought as he did that Mijnheer had treated him unjustly in giving him the poorest of his lands to farm—for was he not, after all, a relative of his wife? That Piet Pienaar thought as he did that nothing more could be done with the van Reenen lands—for had he not here some of the worst soil in the Magerplatz? And that Piet Pienaar thought as he did that Mijnheer was unjust in his expectations and harsh in the demands that he made of his bijwoner. . . .

So, through the drought-cold days, Piet nourished Oom Phanse's discontent until there came a morning when the old man met him at his boundary in a blaze of futile triumph. In his high quavering voice he made it known to the world that he was leaving Mijnheer, his lands and the Magerplatz—all of which, for all he cared, might go to the devil (to whom, as was well-known in Platkops dorp, Mijnheer had long since gone in his youth)—and was going himself, at once and forever, to Princestown to live with a married daughter there. . . .

Though it was for this that Piet had been working, the news of Oom Phanse's decision came to him on that clear cold day as something for which he was not yet fully prepared. For some time he listened unheeding to the old man's rambling talk, and for some time after they parted he wandered restless about his lands, his mind held at one moment by exultation, at the next by anxiety. Only towards evening did he climb heavily up into the loft above the dwelling-house and find his way, in the light of the setting sun, to his hidden canister of gold. Opening it he spread its contents out on the floor, among the pumpkins stored there for winter use, and began laboriously to count up his savings. They came, as well he knew, to within a few pounds of the sum which had last been quoted to him in the Platkops market as the value of the van Reenen lands—and the present drought-parched value of the lands was less than that sum. Twice he went painfully through his reckoning, and again a third time. Stooping over his gold he breathed with difficulty, and exultation and anxiety became blended in an actual physical distress which was new and strange to him and which was far from triumph. In this distress his hands grew cold, clumsy and fumbling. The gold and silver which he was tying now into kidskin bags slipped from his grasp and ran chinkling among the pumpkins. He groped awkwardly after the missing coins and as he groped there came upon him unreasonably, without warning, with a sharp pricking in his spine that was like the ice-cold touch of an enemy creeping upon him from the rear, a sense of almost unendurable loneliness. He stopped short in his hunt and moved uneasily towards the doorway. The sun was setting behind its winter hill and in the chill grey shadows which fell across the yard below him Aantje was driving her hens into their hock for the night. As he watched her there rose within him a desire to call her by name, to speak with her, to escape so from the thrall of his loneliness. But what, if he called to her, should he say? After nearly thirty years of life together he could think of no form of greeting that would not seem strange, and as he pondered she passed out of his sight and Klaas, coming up from the lands, came into it, moving slowly across the earth—tall and gaunt, a part of the rapidly greying landscape, drawn gently into it as he moved, held by it—the one son whom he had begotten, the stranger who dwelt in his house, the toiler who gave his unpaid labour to his land, the reminder always of those other sons whom the Lord had denied him. . . .

Slowly, in the swift piercing chill of winter night-fall, Piet turned from the doorway, gathered together his scattered coins, and tied them up in the kidskin bags. And early next morning, several hours before sun-up, he set off with his small coloured boy in the donkey-wagon for Platkops market and for Mijnheer van Reenen's farm near Platkops dorp.

Andries van Reenen, one of the wealthiest of Platkops farmers was also, because of his hard dealings and his sharp tongue, one of the most feared. Tales were still whispered of the wildness of his youth and his early manhood, but those days were past and only his wealth and power were now spoken aloud. To his bijwoners he was a hard master, and in the market-place, where such things were discussed, only old Oom Phanse's connection with his wife and the acknowledged poverty of the Magerplatz soil could explain his long tolerance of the old man's failure. But in the market-place this had been taken as explanation enough. If Mijnheer had to help a relative whom he knew to be a fool he would certainly not put him in charge of any lands but those he held to be of little value. So it was said in the market-place, and on such talk Piet had built those hopes which brought him now with his savings to the van Reenen homestead. But what neither he nor the men who met in the market-place had realized was Andries van Reenen's increasing passion for growing tobacco wherever he could plant it—and that increasing bitterness of spirit which the slow progress of incurable disease fostered in him and which his wealth and position allowed him to indulge.

When Piet reached the homestead on that drought-cold morning of early winter Mijnheer was sitting on the *stoep* drinking his coffee, and if he was surprised to see his visitor he gave no sign that he was so. He knew Piet Pienaar, of whom lately he had heard much talk from old Oom Phanse, and whose steady progress at Volharding he had watched as he watched all farming in the Platkops district. It was his humour to speak always of Pienaar by the name of his farm. But unlike other men he used 'Volharding' with a certain contempt for the perseverance it betokened. He had, in fact, a greater regard for Volharding's son Klaas than he had for Volharding himself. He knew Klaas, whom he met sometimes at the Platkops market, and with whom, when they did meet, he would always discuss tobacco. And in her youth he had known Aantje.

As Volharding came on to the *stoep* towards him now he greeted him curtly and asked his errand. Without waste of words Piet stated it. He had come, he said, to make Mijnheer an offer for the Magerplatz lands.

'And has it been told to you that I am selling them?' asked Andries van Reenen.

Piet answered that it had not. But, having heard from old Oom Phanse himself that he was giving up the lands and going over the mountains to live with his married daughter in Princestown he had come, as he said, to make Mijnheer an offer.

'And what is the offer that you have come to make?'

Piet named the sum which had been quoted in the Platkops market, and added that what with the continued drought and old Oom Phanse's neglect of the lands this must surely be more than Mijnheer could now expect. His offer was, therefore, thirty pounds less. Two hundred and seventy pounds would he give, and had the money with him here, in gold and in silver, in his wagon-box.

'You rose early, Volharding, to make me this offer for lands that you have many times said to Oom Phanse were worthless,' Mijnheer said grimly. 'But it will not always be drought in the Magerplatz. Presently, while old Oom Phanse sits over the mountains with his daughter in Princestown—saying the things of the Magerplatz lands that you yourself have taught him to say—the rains will come. And what then, Volharding?'

'Mijnheer—' began Piet. But he got no further. Again there came upon him suddenly, with that icy touch as of an enemy tapping his spine, a sense of unbearable loneliness. The cold crept from his spine into the back of his head filling him with unreasonable terror. In that moment he would have cried out for help and friendship even to the grim, ironic, determined and powerful man before him. But he could not cry out. No sign could he give of his agony. And swiftly as it had come upon him it passed and Mijnheer's voice cut harshly into the silence.

'I will tell you what then,' said Mijnheer. 'The man that has my lands in the Magerplatz will plough them and plant them with the tobacco that you swore to Oom Phanse could never be grown there. But that man will not be you. Do you think that because I never came to the Magerplatz I could not see the game you were playing? Was I deaf then, when Oom Phanse came to me with your talk? Or were there two fools in the Magerplatz, Volharding? . . . Was I mad when I spoke with your son Klaas about the lands, and went by what he, and not Oom Phanse, said of them? Or was I right to go by the word of your son? . . . You know well that I was right. You know well that your son Klaas spoke the truth when he said that tobacco could be grown there to profit. And tobacco shall be grown there. Yes, tobacco shall be grown in my lands in the Magerplatz as well as in my lands in the Kombuis—but it shall not be grown by you.'

The harsh voice ceased and for a moment there was silence unbroken. Then Mijnheer, turning with a shrug towards the open door, spoke his dismissal: 'Look you, Volharding,' he said. 'Oom Phanse was a fool. But the man who even now is on his way to my lands from the Kombuis—he is not a fool. When he comes to the Magerplatz it is to your son Klaas that he will listen. And to your son Klaas I will trust him. Wait now a little, and when the tobacco that you said to Oom Phanse could never be grown there stands high and green in my lands come to me again with your gold in your wagon-box. Come to me then, Volharding, and when you come to me then we will speak of it. But now I have finished.'

. . . When, late that night, Piet returned to Volharding, it seemed to Aantje that he had been drinking—but it was not with brandy that he was drunk but with bitterness. He had been a fool, and now knew it, not to remember that though Andries van Reenen had never visited his lands and had left them to a man like Oom Phanse he might refuse to sell them. Yes, Mijnheer had been right, and through all these last years of his labour there had been two fools in the Magerplatz—and he had been the greater. Yet how could he have foreseen Mijnheer's manner of refusal? How could he have guessed that through all these years Mijnheer, giving no sign, had been watching him, playing with him, as he himself had played with Oom Phanse? Why should Mijnheer have watched him? Why should Mijnheer have concerned himself with his affairs? Why should Mijnheer have spoken to Klaas, and never to him, of his Magerplatz lands? Klaas! Klaas!

It was at this point, in his bitter broodings after his return to the farm, that his resentment against Mijnheer gave way to resentment against his son. It was Klaas who, with his foolish talk, had lost him the van Reenen lands. It was Klaas who had robbed him of the just reward of his labour, of the head to his hammer, of the triumph against his God. Yes, through Klaas the God who had denied him his regiment of sons still mocked him. And he could see now no way in which to get even with God. Suddenly all meaning was gone out of his labour, all direction out of his life. He who had been so strong of purpose had now neither purpose nor strength. Though he was not drunk as Aantje had suspected, his thoughts were as loose and sprawling as the limbs of a drunken man, and for many days they remained so. For many days after he had stowed away his gold in the loft—and he stowed it away in the kidskin bags without troubling to replace it in the small tin canister—he was like a man stricken by illness, absorbed in himself and indifferent to the movement and life around him. Not even the arrival of the new bijwoner roused him. The bijwoner's wagon passed close by the Volharding dwelling-house on its way to the house which had once been Oom Phanse's, but Piet in his lands seemed scarcely to note it. It was Klaas who, chancing to be on the road as it went by, opened the gate into Mijnheer van Reenen's lands for it, and, looking up, saw seated upon a feather bed a young woman who smiled gravely upon him over the child she held in her lap. And with that smile life, which was now so empty and meaningless for Piet, began to have a new meaning and riches for his son Klaas.

The bijwoner whom Mijnheer van Reenen had sent to his Magerplatz lands from the Kombuis was a middle-aged widower, Hendrick Mostert by name,

whose wife had died at the birth of his seventh child
and whose niece, Dientje, the young woman in the
wagon, had since kept house for him. Hendrick was
a cheerful capable man, and from the first day of his
arrival with his young family there was noise and
laughter in the bijwoner's house where for so many
years old Oom Phanse had lifted up his voice only in
complaint. The house lay but a short distance from
the Volharding boundary, and just as Piet used
formerly to find his way there by chance to meet old
Oom Phanse, so, within a week of their arrival, Klaas
began to find his way there hoping to come by chance
upon Hendrick and his children, and to catch sight,
in the distance, of Dientje. At these casual meetings
—and soon they ceased to be casual—he was treated
always by Hendrick as an equal, and as a man in
whose judgment on the question of the Magerplatz
soil Mijnheer van Reenen had confidence. By the
children he was hailed as 'Oom' and claimed as a
friend of long standing. But while he talked with
Hendrick and the children it was Dientje, busy
about the house and the yard, whose welcome he
sought from afar.

Dientje Mostert, whose life was spent in consoling
the children of others, was a quiet, orderly, large-
hearted woman of thirty, with no beauty, but that
which lay in her dark brown eyes and soft brown
hair and in the gentle kindliness of her expression.
It was strange to all who knew her that she had never
married, but if she herself regretted this she gave no
sign of it. She gave indeed little sign to the world of
what passed through her mind. Yet what passed
through her mind passed also through her quiet soul
and made her life—so narrow in its setting, so harsh

in its poverty—a gracious one.

It was perhaps this grace and kindliness which drew Klaas so quickly to her. Among such women as he knew none possessed it. But his acquaintance among women was limited, for Piet's miserliness and bitterness, and Aantje's dumb spiritlessness had given poor welcome to those who rarely, and only on some definite errand, had sought the Volharding homestead. And in the market-place at Sacrament time, when young people met together in Platkops dorp, Klaas, with no money in his pocket to spend, no easy talk on his tongue to banter, and a parent who still bought all his clothes for him, had caused no rivalry among those in search of a husband. Nor had he himself ever thought of marriage as within the range of the possibilities of his life. That aloofness of which, in the market-place, young women sometimes complained, was not, as they thought, the aloofness of pride, but the diffident withdrawing of a humble-minded man.

With Dientje, however, there could be neither aloofness nor diffidence. Her smile drew all around her into the gentle warmth of her unspoken friendliness, and to Klaas her coming to the Magerplatz and into his life was like the slow and sure and God-ordained uprising of the sun to a new day. With the simplicity and assurance of a child accepting the inevitable he turned towards her friendship. And as to a child she gave him welcome, widening the circle of children in the bijwoner's cheerful noisy house and drawing him into it.

Quickly, yet to himself with no sense of haste, Klaas's way of life was changed. The bijwoner's children breaking down, in their determination to

reach him, the barriers between Mijnheer van
Reenen's lands and those of Volharding, broke down
other barriers of which they knew nothing. Under
the assault of their clamorous friendship, as in the
benign warmth of Dientje's, he found himself borne
into a new world full of adventure and beauty. In
the cold, clear, drought-idle days which followed the
bijwoner's arrival the very desolation of the Magerplatz grew mysteriously lovely to him, so that often
he would pause in his work to gaze around him upon
the world in wonder. For the Volharding lands he
had never had that narrow, passionate and possessive
love which made Piet blind to any beauty that lay beyond his own boundaries. The green of other men's
lands was never so green to Piet as the green of his
own, but Klaas had looked upon all alike with a
clearer and juster vision. And to his vision now there
came, through Dientje's smile, a radiance that lay
light as the breath and dew of heaven upon all his
drought-parched world.

This radiance shone for him alone. The drought
which Piet had welcomed so grimly was long in
breaking. Day after day clouds gathered above the
Teniquota Mountains only to fade and melt in the
clear bright sky leaving the cold dry air colder and
drier than ever. Anxious men, unable to plough till
the rains came, spent their days tense and brooding,
watching ruin draw slowly nearer. Even cheerful
Hendrick, going with his children and Klaas some
miles down the dried-up river to the last of its water-
holes for drinking-water, began to search for the
cause of the Lord's displeasure, for surely only in
punishment of sin could He so afflict them. And to
Aantje, watching silent from her doorway, it was as

if two men alone in the Magerplatz failed to realize the disaster that was upon them—her son Klaas and her husband Piet.

It was Piet's indifference which disturbed and distressed her most. Klaas's friendship with the bijwoner's children—who came clamouring about the house for him—had nothing in it that was unnatural. Klaas was but a child at heart himself—a child whom circumstance had all his life cut off from friendship with others of his age. And it was not so much to be wondered at that in the play and laughter of the new bijwoner's family Klaas should sometimes forget the devastation of the drought. But for Piet's indifference she could find no excuse that seemed to her natural. She knew nothing of those long-nourished hopes and schemes which had taken Piet to Mijnheer van Reenen's farm near Platkops dorp, and nothing of the interview which had taken place there. She knew only that Piet had returned to her from that journey so strange in his manner that she had thought him drunk, and that he had not been drunk, and that he was still strange in his manner. On that last journey in the donkey-wagon something had befallen him—she could not guess what. And she dare not question him. She dare not try to discover the cause of the trouble that was upon him. She could only watch him in an anxiety which, when at times he realized it, brought his wrath furiously upon her. And slowly, to add to her uneasiness, she became aware that just as she was watching Piet so Piet in turn was watching their son Klaas.

Never, since his interview with Mijnheer at the van Reenen farm, had Piet been able to free his thoughts from their bitter occupation with his son. Against the dark background of his frustrate schemes Klaas stood out for him now in a strange new light, and, blind or indifferent though he was to the havoc wrought around him by the drought, everything that Klaas did seemed to him full of significance. Yet what that significance was he could not easily have said. He knew only that wherever Klaas went there must his gaze follow him. Whatever Klaas said that must he question. Whatever Klaas did that must he criticize. Yet rarely was question or criticism spoken aloud. His brooding resentment found no relief in utterance except when sudden fury seized him and shook him into speech that seemed to his hearers to have no connection in time or place with the matter in hand. In these outbursts he sought fiercely to wound, and so to reach and possess, the mind of his son. But as always Klaas eluded him, protected from his thrusts by that deepening love of Dientje which was now the safe and secret anchorage of his soul.

Of his son's friendship with the bijwoner's niece Piet saw and guessed nothing. It was Klaas's friendship with the bijwoner himself that so bitterly concerned him. As Mijnheer had willed it so now it was. In any difficulty the bijwoner appealed to Klaas for advice and abode cheerfully by that advice. It was indeed as if the van Reenen lands were to be farmed through the new bijwoner by his son Klaas, and for every remembered word or action of Mijnheer and his son, bearing on the part thus set for him by Mijnheer, wild and fantastic explanations now offered themselves to his mind like crazy guests but awaiting a welcome. And to all he gave welcome.

Soon there was no suspicion too unjust for him to harbour. Soon the evil in his own mind touched all his world with evil, and everywhere he sought it, hoarding his finds as jealously as once he had hoarded his gold for the van Reenen lands.

So, at Volharding, the slow and cold and idle days of winter drought slipped by, and Piet, a changed man, moved solitary in a changed and changing world of his own imagining. In this world all were now as alien to him as was his son Klaas—and there came a day when out of his bitter brooding stole the suspicion that Klaas was not his son—that Klaas, the one son whom Aantje had borne, and whose birth had closed her womb to those other sons for whose creating he had married her, was no child of his.

It was after the midday meal, on a day that seemed colder and clearer than all the rest, that Piet made his last evil garnering. Early in the day he had heard Klaas say that he was to go with Hendrick Mostert to search for a new water-hole in the river-bed, and throughout the meal he brooded on this in heavy silence. Then suddenly, without warning of any kind, came one of those dreaded outbursts that had for his wife and son no reference to anything that had been spoken before. Turning towards Klaas he cried in such bitterness and hate that his soul seemed rent with anguish: 'Go then—you that farm for Mijnheer the lands that should have been mine to add to Volharding!' and rising himself from the table left the room and climbed up into the loft where none dare approach him.

It was here that, often now, he sat, hidden himself in the shadow of the doorway, to keep watch on

Klaas's movements. From this angle he looked out
over a fair portion of his own farm of Volharding,
and could see also part of the van Reenen lands, the
line of the river, and the hills and mountains which
bounded his world to the south. As if in a daze he
sat looking out upon this familiar world grown now
in his bitterness so strange to him, and could not
have said whether it was moments or hours that
passed before, tall and spare above the grey earth,
Klaas came into sight walking slowly along the van
Reenen boundary as he himself used once to walk
there hoping to meet Oom Phanse. Yes, there Klaas
went—on his way to meet the new bijwoner. What
was it that they would speak of when they met?
Kombuis tobacco? Was it tobacco alone, and the way
to grow it here in the Magerplatz, that they spoke
of—or did their talk run to other things too? He
could not tell. He could not guess the interests of his
son. He could not read his thoughts. Had not Klaas,
even as a child, been always a stranger to him? Had
Klaas's mind, even as a child, ever been clear to him?
Those unborn sons of his constant brooding had
minds like his own, and in body too were like him—
square and dark and strong. Yes, thick strong men
would they all have been, those sons that he should
have begotten to make known in the world the name
of Pienaar of Volharding! But Klaas? Klaas was no
Pienaar! Where had Klaas got his tall thin body?
None of Aantje's people had been taller than his own,
yet Klaas as he moved among other men in the
market-place in Platkops dorp was tall as a Delport
from the Ghamka or as a van Reenen from Wit-
doornskraal! A van Reenen. . . .

So far his thoughts had run before Klaas passed

out of sight and now in a bitter and exultant harvesting of evil they ran farther. Old Oom Phanse's talk came back to him and eagerly he welcomed it. Though other men, made fearful by his riches and the sharpness of his tongue, might pause before speaking in criticism of Andries van Reenen and the wildness of his youth old Oom Phanse had never hesitated to do so. Not only in his youth, Oom Phanse had declared, but also in his middle age, not only once but many times, had Andries van Reenen gone to the devil and taken a woman with him. And now, alone in his loft, his mind tortured by the bitterness of his own brewing, his body shuddering under the touch of that terrifying unseen enemy whose return came with any violence of emotion, Piet added to old Oom Phanse's list of whispered names one name more— his own wife Aantje's.

Wildly, feverish as a digger who comes suddenly upon treasure of which he fears that reason or authority may presently despoil him, Piet gathered together the suspicions and discoveries of his disordered brain and built up the evil phantasy which rid him of his son. Fool, fool he had been not long ago to have guessed the truth as now he saw it! Did not the truth—that Klaas was no child of his: that Klaas, the hated stranger in his house, the hated stranger in his lands, the foiler of his schemes, the spoiler of his mother's womb and the usurper of his unborn brothers' rights, was no Pienaar of Volharding but the sin-begotten son of Andries van Reenen and his wife Aantje—did not this make all things clear as daylight to him? Did it not explain Mijnheer's interest in Klaas and belief in his word? Why else should Mijnheer be interested in Klaas

and trust to his word? . . . Did it not explain Mijnheer's secret meetings with Klaas? Surely there had
been secret meetings with Klaas when Klaas went
alone to the Platkops market, or how could Mijnheer
have come to form so high an opinion of Klaas
as a farmer of Magerplatz lands? . . . Did it not
explain Mijnheer's determination to stick to his
Magerplatz lands? How else could Mijnheer be
sure of keeping in touch with his son? His son—yes,
there he had it, there he had it, and all things pointed
to it!

It was, strangely, by Klaas and not by Aantje that
his thoughts at first were held, and against Klaas that
his violence of repudiation was directed. He was,
indeed, less concerned to find proof of Aantje's
unfaithfulness than to find proof that Klaas was
Andries van Reenen's son. While of late years his
hatred of his son had become increasingly active and
been brought to something like madness by the
frustration of his plans for buying the van Reenen
lands, his feeling towards his wife had sunk without
forgiveness for her failure to bear him his regiment
of sons, to mere indifference. It was, in fact, almost
with contempt that he sought, in the distant past,
proof that Aantje had gone to the devil with Mijnheer. If there were now secret meetings between
Klaas and Mijnheer had there not been in the past
secret meetings between Aantje and Mijnheer? If
she had known Mijnheer while in service in Platkops
dorp before her marriage had she not known him
afterwards too? Yes, he could see it now. That
change which had come upon her in the early months
of her marriage and which he had taken as victory for
himself had been no victory won by him. It had been

simply the penitence of the sinner which comes from the fear of discovery.

So he read it now—and in that victory that was no victory, in that meekness that was but a secret and fearful repentance, saw himself mocked by his wife Aantje as, through all these years, he had been mocked by Mijnheer in Platkops dorp and by God in heaven. Yes, with Klaas as their single weapon, through all these years of his futile labour, had God and Mijnheer and Aantje mocked him. But they should mock him no longer. Their mockery should cease, and he himself, the first and the last of the Pienaars of Volharding, would end it.

So, in the clear and terrible 'daylight' of his madness Piet came to his resolve.

. . . When he came down from the loft Piet crossed the yard where Aantje was stamping mealies for the evening meal, entered his harness room for a moment, and came out again with his gun. By the side of the mealie-stamper he paused, gazing fixedly at Aantje as if by gazing at her he might force her to read all that was now made clear to him. But in his gaze Aantje could read no knowledge of her sin, for she was innocent of sin: no accusation of mockery, for she was innocent of mockery. She could see only that his strange illness was again upon him—and that she must not attempt to ease him of his distress lest by doing so she should aggravate it. But as she paused in her work, waiting for him to break the silence, her faded eyes filled slowly with unaccustomed tears, and in spite of her effort at restraint a cry was wrung from her: 'Piet, Piet! What is it then, Piet?'

'You know well what it is,' answered Piet. 'But wait now a little and you will know better.'

He said no more, but, turning abruptly, strode out of the yard taking, as Aantje saw, the path towards the van Reenen boundary along which, but a short time before, Klaas too had gone. For some time, in tears for she knew not what, Aantje watched him. At the van Reenen fence he came upon the youngest of the bijwoner's children playing with an old rag ball. She saw him stop and question the child, saw the child point in an upper direction towards the river, saw Piet go on. And now suddenly his purpose, which had for her only madness to explain it, was revealed to her, and flinging down her long wooden stamper she began to run—not after Piet, for in his rapid stride she could not hope to overtake him, but towards the bijwoner's house where surely help for her son would be forthcoming. . . .

At the bijwoner's house it was Dientje alone whom she found—and there, in less than a dozen words, it seemed, in less than a dozen seconds, Dientje had grasped her terror and was sharing it with her. With scarcely a pause in her running, only a change in its direction, Aantje found herself running now towards the river at a lower point than that at which Piet must reach it, and where, said Dientje, she might still find Hendrick and Klaas, who, unknown to the child with the ball, had gone there first to examine an old waterhole. Dientje herself, so much fleeter of foot, would follow Piet by a short cut and so overtake him and somehow convey a warning to Klaas if Aantje had failed to find him. . . .

Fleet of foot though Dientje was, Piet, made swift

by a passion that the very action of striding across the
veld in pursuit of relief to it seemed but to increase,
had reached the drift across the river before she came
within call of him. And now, halting there by a
tremendous effort of will, he sought shelter behind
a crumbling drought-baked pillar of river sand to
await the approach of the bijwoner and his son.
Already he could hear in the distance the children's
voices light and gay in the clear cold air. Soon now
they would be coming round the bend to the drift.
Soon now they would be in a line with his pillar, and
when Klaas reached that line all mockery of him—
Piet Pienaar of Volharding—should cease. Yes, but
a few moments more of this cramped torture of body
and mind must he endure and then would come his
threefold triumph—against Aantje, against Mijnheer, and against God. . . .

So, trembling against the pillar, he awaited Klaas's
coming—and as he waited there came upon him that
sharp prick of the spine, that terrifying pressure at
the back of his head, that deadly grip of the unseen
and inhuman enemy wrought into being by the
violence of his own emotion. Never before had this
inhuman presence been so real to him, or his agony
so great. Never before had it called him by name,
yet now it gave him greeting. From the bank behind
him it came—'Piet Pienaar! Piet Pienaar! What
would you do then, Piet Pienaar?'

He made no answer. He made no movement.
He must be deaf to this interfering voice if Klaas's
voice he would hear—and for Klaas's voice he would
listen. But again came the call, and nearer now—
so near indeed that Piet, in uncontrollable terror,
swung suddenly round, jerked his elbow against

the crumbling sand, lurched forward unsteadily, and fell to the astounding, shattering report of his gun.

When Klaas, running up with the bijwoner, reached the sandy drift Dientje was on her knees by Piet's side. The stricken man looked up at the son who had thus, to the last, eluded him—but speech was beyond him. So, too, perhaps, was hatred. So, too, perhaps, were bitterness and unjust suspicion. But none who watched him could tell what passed then through his mind. In life his thoughts had been secret from them, and so now they were on the threshold of death. All that was known and could afterwards be told was that, with his last conscious movement, it was towards Dientje and away from his son that he turned—and under her compassionate gaze that he closed his eyes upon the world.